W9-DEY-165

Fizz & Riah

Caught By a Boss

A NOVEL BY

TNESHA SIMS

© 2017

Published by Royalty Publishing House
www.royaltypublishinghouse.com

ALL RIGHTS RESERVED

Any unauthorized reprint or use of the material is prohibited. No part of this book may be reproduced or transmitted in any form or by any means, electronic, or mechanical, including photocopying, recording, or by any information storage without express permission by the publisher.

This is an original work of fiction. Names, characters, places and incidents are either products of the author's imagination or are used fictitiously and any resemblance to actual persons, living or dead is entirely coincidental.

Contains explicit language & adult themes suitable for ages 16+

ACKNOWLEDGEMENTS

I really want to thank Royalty Publishing House for all the support and Porscha S. for having faith in me. I want to thank my supporting husband, James, who continues to support my dream. To my sister, Kesha, you have been wonderful. There isn't a time when you haven't been there for me, and I thank you so much for all you do. My brother-in-law, Antonio, I love you so much, and I want you to know that we're down to ride for you, so this one for you, bro. My friends and family, thank you all for the support and love. Larry, I love you, bro, and hope you see this as an eye opener and know there's more to life than the eye can see. Muskegon, I also dedicate this one to you, I put on for my city…. Aye!!!

When God gives you a gift, it's up to you to use it.

FOLLOW ME ON SOCIAL MEDIA

Facebook: @Tnesha Sims

Instagram: @authortneshasims

Twitter: @Tnesha Sims

Dozer

I knew something wasn't right when I woke up this morning. I had this gut feeling that some shit was about to go down. Riah getting kidnapped was a surprise to all of us. Keeping Kiya calm wasn't easy. She was ready for war. I called Fizz right away, but he wasn't answering his phone. I remembered Nikki was picking him up, so I called her. She was just as shocked. She said she was on her way to Fizz's crib and she would tell him then. That shit was two hours ago. Now, neither one of them were answering their phones. Sir was following me, so he wasn't keeping tabs on Fizz's whereabouts. I knew whenever Fizz discovered what happened to Riah, the city of Atlanta was going to bleed red, because he was going to flip the fuck out.

Kiya and I made it to her house. She jumped out the car while it was still moving. Roxy was standing at the door, crying. After I parked the car, I got out, and Roxy started yelling at me.

"Why did you tell me not to call the police? What should I do? I'm going to lose my mind if something happens to my child. I'm going to call the police!" Roxy said as she walked off and grabbed the phone.

"No! We are not calling the police. I have every one of my men on this, but this shit isn't adding up. It's money they want, but a war is what whoever took Riah is going to get. Whoever took her must know someone close to her, personally, because they're going to have to contact the person for the money. Roxy, I know that's your daughter, but lil' man shouldn't be hearing all of this. Take him in the house. Matter of fact, pack y'all bags. I can't have whoever it is back tracking and y'all still here," I said, looking toward Kiya. She had this look on her face. She had fire in her eyes, and I didn't know what she was thinking.

"You straight, baby? We're going to get her back. Just stay focused," I said, and she didn't answer back. Roxy came out of the house with their things. I knew they all were worried, but the police weren't going to help us. I was trying to keep them off our radar, and so far, I'd made sure of that.

I tried calling Nikki again, and she still didn't answer. I was getting worried now, because Fizz always answered his phone. Part of me felt like whoever was gunning for me had something to do with this. *I need to find Fizz, ASAP*, I thought to myself. I brought Kiya, Roxy, and Rico to my house. I let them get settled and was about to walk out when Kiya stopped me.

"I'm going with you, Dozer," she said.

"No, you're not. I need you to stay here and—" she cut me off and looked dead into my eyes.

"That's my fucking cousin, and I want to be there when we find her."

I didn't feel like arguing with her, and I understood that she wanted to be there. I showed Roxy a guest room and showed Rico some games that I had to keep him occupied. Once I locked up, Kiya and I got in my car and drove toward Fizz's house. Sir was still behind me, following my every move.

"So, is that one of your guys following us?" Kiya asked.

"Yes. You're observant, I see."

"Dozer, I know Riah didn't have any enemies, so this has to be some shit with Fizz."

"Kiya, I'm gon' keep it one hundred with you. I think it's the same nigga that is gunning for me," I said, looking at her.

"That shit you told me about… what was his name?" she uttered.

"Some nigga named Tru. I've never heard of him, nor have I seen him, but Fizz mentioned a truck following him. It could be him. I don't know who else it could be."

"So you're telling me that he had someone following him and didn't say shit or warn Riah to be alert?"

"Baby, I know, but we didn't want to alarm you all."

"Dozer, I'm trying to stay calm. You better find Fizz, and fast, because I'm going to start offing motherfuckers if someone doesn't start telling me something. Wait… How do I know it wasn't you and Fizz?"

"What?" I asked, confused.

"You and Fizz! Y'all are probably trying to set some shit up, thinking I'm going to come off the money. Well, you won't see a fucking dime," she said as she pulled her gun out, took the safety off and pointed it toward me.

"Whoa! Are you fucking serious? Kiya, don't fucking point that shit at me," I said, grabbing the gun out her hand and putting it under my seat, all while trying to focus on the road. I looked at her and knew she was just acting out because she didn't know what else to do, but pulling a gun on me was the wrong move.

"Kiya, listen. I know you're scared, but why would I do something like that? I have money. I would never take money from you, or try to get money out of you," I said, trying to assure her that I had nothing to do with Riah getting kidnapped for ransom.

"Oh, but you damn sure took $8,000 from me… took that shit with no hesitation!" she yelled.

"Kiya, I was actually waiting on a good time to give you the money back. I had my accountant write you a check. It'll be from my club, Core, because I hate tracing information back to me. It'll be like I'm paying you for a service that you provided for me. Miss me with that money shit. I'm a fucking boss! Why the fuck would I need a million dollars from a bitch, when I've got triple that shit," I said, letting her piss me off. I should've just kept my cool, but she was pissing me off to the max.

We made it to Fizz's house, and the first person I noticed was this lil' freak I used to fuck with. She worked as a Forensic scientist, and we kept her on payroll for her expertise. I knew she was there for a reason, and I needed to find out what reason that was.

I jumped out the car and walked right behind her as she was walking back into Fizz's house with our maid, Maria. Kiya was right on my heels.

"Kim, what the fuck happened here? Where is Fizz?" I asked, walking up to her as she gathered her things.

"Well… hello, Mr. Edgemen. I think you know what happened here, and Fizz was supposed to be on his way to the hospital, but you know how your brother can be. Your cleanup crew just left, and I was called to make sure nothing was left behind. I did have to clean up a few things, so tell your crew they are getting sloppy," she said.

"Hospital? Is he okay? Please tell me what is going on. Was Nikki with him?" I asked, looking at how thick her ass had gotten. That shouldn't have even been on my mind, but damn.

"He is okay. He was screaming at Nikki, because she made him go seek medical treatment. I'm guessing maybe he's not actually going to the hospital. I'll assume you know where he is going," she commented as she smirked while pulling her glasses off her head.

"I just need a name, Kim," I said.

"Mason! But like I said, tell your cleanup crew to be more careful. Oh… and who is this? The pick of the week?" Kim said, eyeing Kiya.

"Kim, please do not start that crazy shit. We keep you on payroll for a reason," I said, looking into her eyes.

"Yes, well… I'm done here. Maria, it's all yours. Bye, Mr. Edgemen," she said, waving at Maria and passing me.

I rubbed my hands down my face. Mason was dead. I'm guessing he pulled some shit with Fizz, but if Fizz needed medical attention, he must've shot Fizz. The shit wasn't making sense. I called Nikki's phone again and still no answer. I tried Fizz's, and it went straight to voicemail.

"You mind telling me who the fuck that was, and what is going on?" Kiya said, looking at me.

Damn, she was so quiet that I forgot she was even with me.

"Basically, Mason is dead, our cleanup crew that takes care of the bodies left some blood behind, so Kim was called to finish their job, and to make sure nothing can ever get traced back to us. She cleared this motherfucker out good. That's what she does. Kim and I had a thing back in the day, about two years ago. Once we started doing business, I ended it. She's just salty because you're fine and all that good shit, but I need to find Fizz and Nikki," I said, trying to sum it up and hoping she wasn't pressed by Kim saying that shit about being my pick of the week.

"This shit is crazy. I have to find Riah, so take me to my car," she said, walking away.

"You think I don't want to find Riah? That's why I'm trying to find Fizz, so we can piece this shit together. Matter of fact, let's go. I know where he and Nikki are," I said, walking out the house. Maria knew to lock up. She had been in this family long enough to know how we got down.

I was slipping. I needed to focus and think smart. I wasn't thinking, though. I should have known where Fizz was, but it was like something was distracting me.

We were driving toward my mom's house. If Fizz wasn't going to the hospital, he was going to our mom's house. Our mom was a nurse for over twenty years, and she specialized in wound care. So many thoughts were going through my mind. I knew Mason wasn't shit. I looked over at Kiya, and she had tears coming down her face.

I started thinking about Riah and how she was going to miss her high school graduation. I knew she was probably scared, wherever she was.

"Kiya, I am so sorry this happened to Riah, and I promise you, we are going to do everything in our power to get her back."

She didn't respond. I didn't pressure her to talk. I made it to my mom's house, and Nikki's car was there. We walked in, and we heard a lot commotion coming from my mom's bathroom.

"*I*'m going to turn this fucking city out. Whoever gets in my fucking way is going to die. I don't give a fuck," I yelled, more at Nikki. I should be happy my sister saved my life, but I wasn't happy that she grazed my damn ear, damn near taking my fucking ear off. If I wasn't losing so much blood, I would have said fuck it and continued to look for Riah…

Mason was just about to pull the trigger on me when Nikki walked up behind him and shot him three times, once in the head, and twice in the neck, but one went right through and grazed my ear.

I wasn't going to the damn hospital, so Nikki drove me to our mom's. I was fucking seeing red. Nothing anyone said made sense, and as soon as my mom fixed me up, I was going on a hunt.

I looked up to see Dozer and De'Kiya walking in. I could just imagine what she was going through, and her eyes told it all.

"Man, what the fuck. I've been calling y'all, nonstop," Dozer yelled.

"Man, your sister's no aiming ass grazed my damn ear, trying to shoot at that nigga Mason," I said, getting pissed again about my ear and the fact that my girl was kidnapped.

"Fuck you, Fizz. My aim saved your fucking life," Nikki said, getting up and noticing Kiya.

"Kiya, I am so sorry. I hope Dozer assured you that we have our men on the hunt as we speak," Nikki said, hugging Kiya.

"Yo, Nikki, what happened?" Dozer asked.

"Mason tried to kill Fizz. I got there just in time. Apparently, his brothers from up North sent him y'all way. I have his phone and read all his messages. They're actually on their way here. After him not responding, they said if he doesn't respond in the next hour, they were coming," she said.

"I told you that nigga was a snake, didn't I?" Dozer asked.

"Okay, let's calm down. We do have a guest that I have yet to meet," our mother said, as she finished cleaning Fizz's wound up.

"My fault, mom. This is De'Kiya, my girlfriend. Riah is her cousin," Dozer said, looking at our mother.

"Well, it's nice to finally meet you, and I am so sorry about Riah. My prayers are with you. My name is Joyce Edgemen. Now, I don't agree with my children's lifestyles, but one thing I know is that they will find Riah," she said.

"Thank you," Kiya said.

After our mother excused herself, we started coming together. If Mason was at my house, then whoever that nigga, Weedie is, must have Riah.

I changed my shirt before we left, because it had blood on it from my ear. We went to the warehouse where we held most of our street meetings. That nigga, Ant, said he was still working on a first name for that nigga, Weedie. I looked down at my phone, and I had twenty-one missed calls. Two of those were from the prison where Nazir was.

Apparently, they extended his time for two more weeks, because he pushed a guard head for talking slick to him. I knew he probably tried calling Dozer and Nikki, also.

I just wanted my girl. I know she was scared. Whoever that nigga, Weedie, was… he was a dead man walking. I was tired of playing with this nigga, Ant. He had so much information but couldn't get a first name for shit. I walked up to him with my gun and pointed it to his head.

"You've got ten seconds to get me a first name from your cousin, or you're just as dead as that nigga, Weedie," I demanded. I was done playing with these niggas.

"Okay, man. Let me get my phone. I'll get it," Ant said, damn near crying.

I watched him call his cousin. He talked him into asking his girl what Weedie's real name was. After a few minutes, the name Chris came through Ant's speaker phone. Kiya was already running out the door. Dozer and Nikki were right on her heels. I told Ant to end the call. Killa was going to keep an eye out on his bitch ass. He was starting to look real suspect.

Chris

I finally got that stuck up bitch. I had to make it seem like a graduation prank. Otherwise, Mo wouldn't have helped me snatch Riah up. I must admit that she was looking gorgeous for graduation, but money was the only thing on my mind. When that nigga, Tru, asked for my services, and told me it was a half of a million dollars involved, I couldn't resist. I really didn't have a problem with Riah, but when she became my victim, the hatred toward her just built itself...

Riah was just about to get into that nigga Fizz's car when Mo and I grabbed her. She put up a good fight. I didn't know she was that strong, I heard she could get down with them hands, but damn. She almost knocked Mo's head off, swinging at him. We had on masks so that no one could see who we were. We had to tape her mouth, because she was talking reckless.

"Man, graduation is in less than thirty minutes. Joke is over. I've got to get to the arena," Mo said.

"Okay, man. Go ahead," I voiced.

"Okay, are we going to untie her now? I'm sure her family is worried sick, and she needs to get to the arena for graduation."

"Man, look. This shit is deeper than what I told you. I was ordered to do a job, and I did it. Now let's roll. And I'm gon' need you to keep this shit on the hush. If you can do that, then I'll throw you twenty racks for your trouble," I specified.

"Wait, what? You're telling me this shit was for real? We kidnapped her on some real shit? Man, I don't want no parts of this shit. I've got a football scholarship. I can't jeopardize that for $20,000. Chris, you know I've been down to ride for you on a lot of shit, but this… I can't fuck with."

I looked at his soft ass and knew he would bitch up. That's why I couldn't tell him the truth until after we grabbed her.

"Look here, you can get ghost, but you better not ever speak on what went down here. Once Tru comes to get her, she's gon' be his problem. I knew you were going to bitch up, and here I was thinking you had the heart," I hissed.

"Boy, let's get one thing straight. I got the heart. Never have I ever been a bitch. I'm man enough to know this shit ain't right. That's our fucking classmate. Why the hell would you pull some shit like that? When your ass gets caught, that scholarship you're riding is going to be gone," he voiced.

I knew Mo wasn't afraid of me which is why I had my gun ready. His ass was about to come at me correct, and respect what I was doing. Little did he know, I wasn't planning on attending college. I had some shit going on with Tru, which was going to get me paid.

"Nigga, I'm not pressed about no damn scholarship, Fuck College! I'm about to make this money. You can do what the fuck you want, but I got shit to handle."

"So what are you going to tell Mina? You know she is going to be looking for Riah, and not to mention, I don't want any problems with that nigga, Fizz," he mentioned.

"Now we're getting to the truth. You're afraid of that nigga, ain't you? Is that why you let him take Riah from you, talking that tough shit to me? But you didn't get at him about your 'supposed to be' girl, right?" I said, trying to mess with his head.

"No, I'm fucking smart. That's a battle not even you can fuck with. Whoever this Tru nigga is, is going to get you killed, Chris. I advise you to let Riah go. Matter of fact, I'll do it," he said, trying to walk toward the basement where we had Riah hid and tied up.

"Nigga, is you fucking stupid? Get the fuck on, and fuck Fizz. Who the fuck worried about him? I'm not. You want to advise something. Well, let me advise you to get the fuck on, attend graduation, and keep your mouth shut. If I have to tell you again, it won't be with words," I said, eyeing him and daring him to try something.

It seemed as though he took me as a joke, so I pulled my piece out, watching him eye it. If he thought I was playing, he knew I was serious now. I saw his jaw clench. He looked at me and walked away. He was smart... smart enough not to fuck with me. I watched him get into his car and take off. I tried calling Tru again, but he wasn't answering. He hated talking on the phone, so I decided to text him to see if I got a response.

Me: Man, what's up, I told you I got shit to handle on my end.

Tru: Where you at?

One thing about me was that I wasn't a fool. I didn't know for sure if it was Tru who was texting back. Maybe shit went bad on his end, and now, I was being set-up. I needed to make sure it was him.

Me: I need to make sure your head is right. What happened at the spot? You the man now or what?

Tru: If you're asking if Fizz is dead? Yes, that nigga gone... 3 shots to the head. Now where the hell are you?

Me: You know where the hell I'm at... been waiting here for your ass. Your brother, Dre, has been blowing my phone up, looking for you. I told them you probably were fucking that bitch, Nikki. They said they will be rolling in tomorrow, so you better hit them up.

Tru: I didn't ask you to tell me where I think you're at. Where the hell you at, nigga?

Me: Man, is you serious? I'm at the spot you told me to bring Riah. I'm ready for this shit to be over.

Tru: How is she doing?

Me: Who, Riah? She was straight last time I checked on her... not a hair out of place like you asked.

Tru: Good, see you in a bit

Me: Make sure you have my money. I'm out when you get here. I did my part.

Tru: Oh, I got you, I'm going to take care of you. Don't even worry about that.

I looked at my phone. The graduation ceremony was sure to start soon. Mina was going to ask why I didn't attend, but fuck it. They could just mail my shit. I was just happy to be done, anyway.

I walked downstairs to the basement. I didn't have my mask on. I wanted her to see who I was. It's not like Tru was going to let her live, anyway. The house we were at was some chick named Arielle's. From what I heard, Arielle was someone who used to mess with Fizz. When she found out he was messing with Riah, she didn't hesitate to let us use her house. It wasn't like it was anything spectacular, anyway. She had dishes everywhere, clothes all over the floor, and it smelled like rotten eggs. I took the garbage out just so I was able to breathe in the damn house. That shit was so foul. Tru told Arielle to stay away for a few days. He gave her a few stacks, and that bitch got ghost. For her to be so concerned about what Fizz had going on, she sure was trying to give Mason the pussy.

Fizz's lil homie, Ant, put us up on game. We needed a little help to get at Fizz, so he directed us toward Arielle. That bitch told his life story. Tru gave her a few stacks, and she was down for whatever, as long as she got to walk away with Fizz. What we didn't tell her was that Fizz was gon' be dead when she returned.

Once I made it downstairs, Riah started moving around. I can tell she was scared, but I didn't have much sympathy for her.

"Riah Walts, the prettiest girl I know," I said, getting close to her, and she tensed up. She tried talking, but I had scotch tape over her mouth. I ripped it off to see what she had to say.

"Why are you doing this Chris? I haven't done anything to you," she cried.

"It's not personal, baby… only business. I'm sorry you have to miss graduation, but we can't always get what we want," I said.

"Chris, please let me go, and I'll tell Fizz to take it easy on you."

"Ha-ha! Fizz is dead."

I watched her eyes grow wide.

"Fizz is not dead. I know he's not."

"Riah, how can you be so sure? Well, I'm sorry to be the one to tell you, but he died. Three shots to the head, to be exact."

"Why? Who killed him? What do you want from me?"

"Do you have a half of a million dollars? If so, I'll let you go right now," I asked, knowing damn well she didn't. I used to eavesdrop on her and Mina's conversation. I knew her mama was a crack head, so I knew she didn't have any damn money.

"I will get it, if you just let me go. I promise, I'll get you the money."

"Riah, who the fuck you think you fooling?" I asked, looking at her. She looked really sexy. The dress she had on was rising, and I got a nice view of her thighs.

"Chris, please! I've already missed graduation. I promise I won't tell anyone this happened. Just let me go. Who else is in on this?" she asked.

"Mo! He actually put this shit together. At first, I tried to stop him. I told him you were our classmate and that you didn't deserve this, but when we were offered that money, we couldn't refuse."

"I don't understand. Why me, though?"

"Look…. stop with the questions, Riah. Shit, you making me nervous," I said, walking off.

I hated when people questioned me. Shit made me nervous as fuck. I was growing impatient. Tru's ass was taking too long for me. I started to wonder if Mo would go back running his mouth, but I knew he wouldn't. He wanted no parts of this shit. Then, it hit me. I needed an alibi just in case shit went bad. My graduation gown was in the car. I quickly shut the door to the basement, putting the lock back on and headed out the house. I quickly texted Tru back, telling him I needed to at least show my face at the graduation.

Mina

I was so excited when I woke up this morning to attend graduation, but my man, best friend, and Mo were all MIA. I left my phone with my mom, so I couldn't even try calling them again. I was expecting to meet them here. It was my turn to receive my diploma. I just couldn't focus. I was so worried. It didn't make sense. Where could they be?

A few more names were called before I heard Mo Summers. I looked up, and he was walking across the stage. His family was screaming, clapping, and cheering him on. I was hoping Riah and Chris appeared out of nowhere, also. Chris' last name was Wilson, and Riah's was Walts, so their names would be called toward the end. I was consistently turning around, seeing if I could see them. The girl next to me was flicking it up with selfies. I leaned over and asked if I could use her phone to call Riah. She looked at me funny for a minute and then said yeah. Riah's phone rang and rang, so I called De'Kiya's phone next.

"Mina, OMG! Riah has been kidnapped, and Chris is the one who took her," she yelled through the phone.

My world stopped! The voices I heard from the ceremony discontinued. I couldn't focus any more. I didn't want to think it was true, but I knew Deedee, and the tone in her voice had me believing it was true. It made sense. I wondered if Mo was in on it. I wanted to know why. Why would he do that to my best friend? What was his motive? At that moment, I was so happy I got that abortion. I couldn't imagine bringing a child into the world and letting it call him daddy.

"Deedee, are you here at the graduation, I don't know where Chris is. I haven't seen him?" I asked quietly into the phone.

"I'm outside. I was wondering if he was there. Mina, I need your help on this."

I already knew I needed to leave. I told Deedee I would meet her outside in a bit. I didn't want to make as scene, so I stayed calm. My heart was beating so fast. I gave the girl next to me her phone back. I eased out of my seat, trying not to draw too much attention. I walked toward the opposite side. Once I made it outside, Deedee called me over to Dozer's car. I couldn't see who else was in the car with her, because his windows were tinted black. It was another car behind them which I knew to be Fizz's. Deedee told me to get in. Once I got in, I saw that it was her and Dozer.

"Deedee, how do you know this? How you know Chris kidnapped Riah?" I asked while my eyes started to tear up.

"It's a long story, Mina, but the short version is that he started texting Mason's phone. You remember Nikki's boyfriend… or ex-boyfriend?" she asked, and I shook my head yes.

"Well, he tried killing Fizz. It was a whole set-up, and they're holding Riah for ransom," Deedee said, sounding like she was about to cry now.

"What? How much? You know my parents will pay for whatever is it," I said while crying, trying to keep it together.

"It's not the money that's the problem, sweetheart. It's the location we need to figure out—"

"Look, look! There goes Chris right there," Kiya said, interrupting Dozer. She was about to jump out the car when Fizz walked up and shut it back.

"Kiya, I know you want this nigga dead just as much as I do, but we have to be smart. He's sneaking in this bitch, probably trying to find you, Mina. We're going to watch him and follow him. Hopefully, he'll lead us to Riah. If not, we got something that'll make him talk," Fizz said as he slid in the back seat.

"Okay, but I want to be the one to pull the trigger," Deedee said.

I was becoming scared. My parents were criminal defense attorneys. I heard all the time how they handled murder cases. I didn't want Deedee to be one they had to represent, but the streets talk, and I knew Fizz and Dozer were not to be fucked with. I also didn't want to see Chris die, but Riah meant the world to him. If I had to choose, it would be him instead of her.

"Hell no, Kiya. Let me and Fizz handle this. You are not going to be anywhere near his bitch ass," Dozer said, looking at her.

"Kiya, he's right. We can't let you in on this," Fizz added.

"I just want my cousin. I don't have the energy to argue with you all. That nigga is right inside of this building. What are we going to do?" Deedee asked. Nikki opened the door, and I scooted over to the middle. It was quiet, and I could tell everyone was in deep thought.

"What's up? We gon' make this nigga disappear, or what?" she asked, as if she killed for a living. I was starting to think their whole family was some killers.

"Sis, Kiya wants to be the one," Dozer said.

"Okay, let her, if that's what she wants. Don't get in the way of that. Riah is her family. You know how I get about y'all. She only feels that way about Riah. If she wants his blood on her hands to make her sleep better at night, don't take that away from her," Nikki said.

"Okay, wait a minute. We can't just be talking like this in front of this girl," Dozer mentioned.

"Oh, we don't have to worry about Mina. Do we, Mina?" Nikki asked me. Now I wasn't scared, but I wasn't about to play with this crazy family, either.

"Hell nah. My lips are sealed. That's my friend… my heart. What needs to be done is done," I commented back.

"Good, that settles that," Nikki said, leaning back in her seat.

I was sitting in the back of Dozers car, wondering if Riah was scared. I'm sure she was. Once I got her, she was going to move in with me. Her crack head mama couldn't even protect her.

My fucking ear was still hurting. I still couldn't believe Nikki grazed my ear. I guess I'd have to apologize for cursing her out later. I mean, she did save my life. I was slipping big time. I was usually on point with shit like that. It's crazy that my sister's boyfriend tried killing me. I wondered how Nikki was really taking that shit. I knew she had to feel some type of way. I'd have to kick it with her one on one after this shit was over. I knew we needed a solid plan, since Mason's brothers were on their way to my city. I wanted to make sure I greeted them properly.

"So what exactly do y'all need me to do?" Mina asked.

I looked at her. She was willing to ride for her friend, and for that, she gained my trust.

"Mina, I'm going to need you on point. I need you to get with Chris. Once you leave here, my man, Sir, will follow y'all. Just in case he loses y'all, you have to make sure you stay on him. Being that Riah is your best friend, Mina, you're going to have to make it seem like you're worried that she didn't attend graduation. I need you to let him know that you know that Riah has been kidnapped. See how he is going to play this shit out," I said.

"Okay, well… I better get back in there. I'll keep you guys posted," she said as Nikki let her out.

"Kiya, you and Dozer go in, also. Act like y'all are looking for me and Riah," I mentioned to them. Chris didn't know Mason was dead, nor did he know I was still alive. By him seeing Kiya, Dozer, and Nikki, it wouldn't alarm him.

I got back into my own car as they made their way inside, and I laid my head back on the headrest. I wanted my baby to know that I was going to find her and protect her. She was tough, but I knew she had to be scared, not knowing what could happen to her.

Dozer had his ear piece on so that I could hear everything that was said around them. About another half hour went by. I heard Kiya ask Mina if she had seen Riah. Mina was acting her ass off. I had to give it to her. I heard my brother say that Riah and I must be somewhere together, because I wasn't there, either. That's when I heard his bitch ass voice…the voice I was going to torture. Chris told Mina he had to go. She said she was going with him. He didn't say anything, so I assumed they left together. I heard my brother talking. A few minutes later, Chris and Mina walked out. She hugged a woman and a man, who I assumed to be her parents. I watched Chris drive right past me. That shit was so hard to do. I wanted to kill him, but I had to be patient. Sir pulled off, following them.

Dozer and them came back to their cars and drove off. He was headed back to his house. Sir called me up and said Chris and Mina stopped at Red lobster. This nigga had the audacity to be out eating like he didn't have someone kidnapped. I mentioned it to Dozer. Mina had to play the part, and she was doing a hell of a job.

Mina texted Kiya, saying that Chris was acting weird, and trying to make it seem like he had to take care of some things. She said she told him that she wanted to spend the day with him. Mina texted, saying she didn't know how long she could keep him around her, because he was becoming angry and telling her that she was acting too clingy. I told Kiya to tell her that if she thinks he will put hands to her, as I knew he had before, then let him leave. Sir was on him.

Once we made it to Dozer's house, Roxy ass was asking a thousand questions. I guess I couldn't be that mad at her. What could she have done anyway to stop Chris from taking Riah? He probably would've tried to hurt her, also. I went into one of Dozer's rooms and waited on the call for the location when Nikki walked in.

"Bro, I just want to apologize. I was being dumb over a nigga that played the hell out of me," she said.

"Nikki, no need for all of that. Just play it safe next time. How you holding up? I know this shit is fucking with you," I asked her.

"You know me, lil' bro. I'm good," she answered back.

"Nikki, you don't have to be tough all the time. It's okay to show your feelings. You keep trying to hide shit, and it's going to fuck with you in the long run, just like that shit with you and Naz," I said, smiling. She didn't think I knew that she and Nazir had something going on. Dozer didn't, but I did.

"What? I don't know what you mean," she said, trying to play it off.

"Nikki, come on, sis—" I was interrupted by my phone.

"What up?" I asked Killa.

"Man, Sir following him now. He's dropping Mina off as we speak," he said. As soon as Killa said that, Kiya came in. She said that Mina just called and said Chris was dropping her off.

"Okay, we're 'bout to get out here. We still need to prepare for Mason's brothers, but Riah is my main priority right now," I informed Killa.

"I got you," he said, as he ended the call.

I got up to find Dozer when I walked past the room Rico was in. He was praying that God brought his sister home. That shit touched my heart and pissed me off at the same time. I was going to do major damage to Chris.

"Hey, lil' man. Riah is going to be okay. Matter of fact, I'm going to get her now," I told him.

"Okay, Fizz. Where is she? Did she really get kidnapped?"

I didn't like the fact that Roxy was so open to talking around her son about everything under the sun. Some things you just didn't let little kids hear.

"She's good, lil' man. I promise when I bring Riah back, me, you, and her will go somewhere fun," I said.

"Okay, because it's been boring around here."

I had to laugh at him. He was something else. I left him and got Dozer. Dozer and I decided that we were going to leave Kiya and Nikki behind. We snuck out, passing them in the kitchen. I knew they were going to be mad as hell when they found out we left without them.

"Man, Ant was in on this shit the whole time," Dozer said.

"I knew his ass was starting to act differently. That's the envious shit. That nigga acts like he wasn't eating good. Now his momma is gon' be planning his funeral," I revealed. Killa found out that Ant was in on Mason trying to get at us.

"Damn, this is Naz calling," Dozer said as he answered the call. I knew once Dozer told Naz about what was going down, it was going to piss him off, especially the shit about Nikki. I drove toward the warehouse while listening to Dozer tells Naz about what's been going on. My brother wasn't any fool, so of course he was using street codes.

I was five minutes away from the warehouse. I started thinking about my baby again. She was so feisty, smart, and sexy. She talked about being a chef all the time. I couldn't wait for her to be up in our new home, cooking up some shit. Yeah, I wasn't planning on going back to my crib, especially after Mason being killed there. I knew Riah wouldn't want to stay there anyway after that. I really loved that house, though. It was secluded from everyone and everything, but shit... I could find another one just as easy. I actually plan to have Maria's daughter, Francine, to look for another one for me. She was a realtor, and she helped all of us find the houses we currently lived in. She was happy that we helped her mother move here from Mexico, so she found us a great house and made sure we got a great deal.

My phone started ringing, bringing me out of my thoughts.

"What up? Tell me what I need to hear," I replied.

"Get to Arielle's house, now."

That was all that Killa said before he hung up. I busted a U-turn, causing Dozer to react. He looked over at me, crazy.

"That was Killa. He said to get to Arielle's house. I'm not sure why, but he sounded like it was serious," I confessed.

"Arielle? What the fuck? You don't think…?" he asked.

"Shit, I don't know. Soon as we get there, we will find out."

I didn't know what to think. Maybe something happened to Arielle. Chris and Mason probably had gone after her too.

We pulled up to Arielle's house. I called Killa, and he said to come in the back of the house. Dozer and I got out and walked toward the back. We met Killa, and we walked into the house together.

"Man, what's going on?" I asked. He pointed to Arielle's bathroom door. I was confused as to why he pointed to the damn door. Was Arielle there? Was she dead? Shit, I didn't know what to think.

"Riah is in there. Sir followed Chris here. We didn't have time to call you because he walked in and came right back out. We had to make a move fast, bro. We brought him right back in here. He didn't even hesitate to tell us she was in the basement. When she saw me, she got scared, thinking I had a part in this. Once I let her loose, she ran away so fast. I tried to calm her down, but she started swinging, hitting me in my damn eye. She ran into the bathroom. I didn't want to break the door down and scare her even more, so I called you," he said.

"So why is Riah here? Is Arielle here?" Dozer asked, and I was wondering the same thing.

"No! Arielle is not here, but she apparently told Mason a lot about you. Chris mentioned that Mason paid her to get out of sight for a while. I already did a perimeter check. The neighbors are on vacation, and the other house has been vacant for years now, so no one has seen or heard anything."

I laughed to myself. Arielle knew better. Usually, I would get Nikki to handle a female, but Arielle made this shit very personal. I could just imagine what Riah was thinking. First, Killa came to her house looking for her mom. Now, he was here. I had to make sure I said all the right things.

"Where is that nigga?" I asked Killa.

"He in the basement, tied up. You want us to take care of him?" he asked.

"Nah, I got plans for him. I don't want him to see me just yet. Did y'all mention I was still alive?" I asked.

"Nope, I knew you probably had a plan, so we didn't mention it yet."

"Good… get him to the warehouse. I'll be there later. I want him and Ant side by side," I hinted, letting him know how I was going to kill the both of them.

"What you want us to do about Arielle?" Killa asked, and Dozer looked at me, probably wondering the same thing.

"I'll handle her on my own time. Let her stay where she is. We have Mason's phone. She'll probably try to contact him. I'll make my move when the time is right," I told them.

"Alright, well hurry up and handle that with your girl. I'm gon' stick around until y'all leave. Sir will handle Chris," Killa said.

I knocked on the bathroom door, and Riah screamed, "Leave me alone!"

"Riah… baby, it's me. Open the—"

I didn't even get to finish what I was going to say because she swung the door open and ran into my arms. She hugged me so tightly, and I hugged her back.

"You okay, baby?" I asked.

"Yes… No…I missed graduation. Chris and Mo did this. WHY?" she yelled, as tears ran down her face.

"Riah, you're safe. That's all that matters," I assured her.

"No, I'd rather they just killed me. Graduation was the most important day of my life, and I missed it. Nothing in my life has been the way I wanted it to be, so why do I even have a reason to live anymore. My life will never be great. I'll always have something that holds me back."

I hugged her tight and kissed her. No one should ever feel they'd be better off dead. This shit was fucking with me mentally. Usually, I would have something positive to say, but I just wanted to take her pain away.

"Sis, you don't mean that, because I know a little guy that loves you more than anything. You're smart as hell. You have a big brother now that has grown to love you dearly. De'Kiya loves you more than life itself. Now, you have someone who loves, cares, and worships you," Dozer said, pulling Riah into a hug.

"Thanks, Dozer. I love you guys so much," she said.

"But you love me more, right?" I asked, joking around.

"Yes, Fizz," she smiled with tears coming down her face.

We left, heading to Dozer's house. Dozer called Nikki, letting them all know we had Riah. He didn't call Kiya. He knew she was pissed off. Shit, I knew she was pissed. She called our phones back to back. Roxy called, asking to talk to Riah.

"Yes, mom. I'm okay… Yes, I'll be there in a few minutes… No, he didn't hurt me… Yes, mom. Love you, too."

She hung up.

We talked the whole way there. I asked her what she knew, and I told her what I knew about Chris and Arielle. She mentioned it was two guys and said Mo might have been the other guy, because Chris said it was Mo's idea to kidnap her. Mina had mentioned Mo was at the graduation, and that he had actually walked to receive his diploma.

"We will get Mo. Don't worry, baby," I said.

We thought Nikki was calling again, but it was Mina calling from her phone. This meant they were all together. Riah talked to Mina and basically answered the same question she answered for her mom.

"So Mo was there? Chris said that it was Mo's idea," I heard Riah saying to Mina. I looked at her in the rearview mirror. She was so beautiful. I couldn't wait to tell her she was moving in with me. I wasn't asking, because I'd already made it up in my mind that she was.

"I don't know, Mina. When I get there, we can call him and see if he answers."

She ended the call, and we made eye contact through the mirror.

She smiled that beautiful smile, and I smiled back. I wanted this shit to be over and behind us. I also couldn't wait until she was riding my dick. We had sex a few more times after her prom, but my schedule was so full that I didn't get to see her as much as I would have liked. That's why I wanted to get away after her graduation and take her to Vegas, but this shit happened.

"Man, pay attention to the road. If you wanted to stare at her, you should have asked me to drive—"

Dozer didn't finish his sentence because a car ran into us from behind.

"Yo, what the fuck?" Dozer asked to no one in particular. He rubbed the back of his head because he jerked forward then back pretty hard.

"Riah, you okay?" I asked.

"Yeah, my head hit the seat, but I'm fine," she mentioned.

The car that hit us pulled up to the side of me. The car was a black Denali with tented windows, so I couldn't see who was in it. They couldn't see us either, because my shit was also tented. I rolled my windows down an inch to see if they would do the same. They did, but what I saw was a gun pointed at me. I smashed the gas of my Lamborghini, and whoever was in the truck started shooting at us. Riah was screaming. I told her to stay down. I never really speed raced in my car, but one thing I knew was that it had major horse power. I looked back, and they were still following us, but they weren't doing a good job of keeping up.

"Man, even if we lose them, we still don't know who they are. It could be Mason's brothers," Dozer said while holding onto the door with one hand and his gun in the other.

31

"Those niggas couldn't have found us that fast," I said, but then I thought about it. Ant could've put them on what I drove, and how we operate.

"Shit, man. Who else could it be?' he asked. I was trying to concentrate on the road and think at the same time while Riah was screaming.

"Well, make the call," I told him. He wasted no time.

"Killa... man, we need you—"

"I'm already on it. You should put a little more distance between yall, and you got a good lead on them, but hit that shit one time, Fizz," Killa said, cutting Dozer off. I switched gears, adding more speed. I looked in the rearview mirror, waiting for whatever Killa had going on to happen. One thing about Killa was that he was always on us, watching our every move.

"Fizz, are they still following us?" Riah screamed, still lying down.

"Yes, but not for long, got damn!" I said, watching the truck blow up in flames. I didn't see what hit them. I can just imagine what Killa had. That nigga was dangerous with his tools.

"Damn, what the fuck he hit them with... a missile?" Dozer asked.

"Shit, I don't know," I said, slowing down as I turned the car around, heading back toward the truck. We drove closer to the truck, and Killa pulled up. I looked at him, he looked at us, and started cheesing. His ass loved shit like this.

"Yo, look," Dozer said, pointing at a nigga crawling out the car. His ass was burnt the fuck up, but we needed him to live to find out who the fuck he was.

Killa popped his truck and grabbed his gloves. He grabbed the nigga and pushed him inside of the back of his trunk, pouring a gallon of water on him. It was a good thing we were in the middle of nowhere, and it was getting dark. Our clean-up crew pulled up and went to work. They started putting the fire out.

"Okay, let's get his ass fixed up, because we need answers," I sighed.

I felt like I had enough on my plate with Chris and Ant. Now this, and I still had to find Arielle and get at Mo. My brother was letting me take over, and I wanted to make sure I showed him I could handle the shit.

I dropped Riah off at Dozer's house with the ladies and her mom. Rico was so happy to see her. Roxy's ass started crying and praying. Kiya showed Riah how happy she was that she was safe, but she was pissed at Dozer. Mina asked about Chris, and that's when it got quiet. They all wanted to know what was going to happen.

#

I couldn't believe that Arielle was in on that shit with Riah. I knew she was a snake from the beginning. I was happy Fizz got rid of her ass. We had a lot of shit to handle, but Kiya was making it hard for me. I knew she was pissed, but I couldn't let her roll with us. The lifestyle we lived was dangerous. Although I was growing to really love her, until I was out the streets for good, it may be best if I left her alone until then.

After Mina asked about Chris, I looked at Fizz. Not only did we have to tell them about Arielle, but also the truck that was shooting at us.

"Chris was still alive. We wanted to get Riah here safe and out of harm's way. We also have another problem on our hands."

I looked back to see if Rico was still in my guest room. When I saw that he was, I continued.

"Someone ran into us and started shooting at us, but they are all dead now, except one, and we have to find out who he is. We think that it may be one of Mason's brothers," I said.

"Oh, I'm riding out with y'all," Nikki said, grabbing her phone off the table.

"Nikki, I need you to stay with them," I said.

"Dozer, if anyone should be there, it should be me. I'm not some damn rookie, nor am I a babysitter.

"Sis, please don't argue with me right now. We've got to go, and I need you to listen for once. Can you at least do that?" I asked.

She rolled her eyes and walked off. My sister was savage, I wasn't afraid for her to roll out with us. She could definitely handle her own. I just needed her there to protect and watch them. She knew that's why I wanted her there.

"Fizz, let me holla at you before you go," Riah said.

They walked off, and I looked over at Kiya. I guess Mina knew I wanted to talk with Kiya, so she got up and left the room, also.

"Before you even start to say whatever the fuck you are going to say, let me just say this. You knew I wanted to be there for my cousin. Now, you got all this other shit going on. You know Rico and Riah mean the world to me, and I will protect them with all cost."

"I know that, baby. I just wanted to—"

"Look, Dozer, I'm taking my family to Augusta tonight. Mina's mom said we can go there for a while."

"Mina's mom… what the fuck?" I asked.

"Yes, Roxy told her everything. She didn't have anything to say about you or your family. She just said that we needed to get away before anything bad happens."

"So you mean to tell me that Roxy ran off and told Mina's mom, about my family and how we get down?" I said yelling.

Fizz walked back into the living room. He looked at me, and I told him what Kiya just told me.

"I could care less about what y'all doing, but Riah ain't going no fucking where," he announced.

"Riah can speak for herself, and if my family is going, then I am also. I didn't sign up for this shit. I have a brother to take care of," Riah said.

"I am capable of taking care of my son," Roxy said, coming into the room.

"No you're not. As a matter of fact, you have been acting a little weird lately. What... you back on drugs again? Ain't no way in hell you taking my brother in," Riah yelled.

"I'm not on drugs. I wanted to surprise you guys with the house I got. I also met someone. That's why I've been acting weird and sneaking in late nights," Roxy said.

"You met someone? You sound fucking crazy. That right there tells me you don't get it. Rico should be your main priority, not some damn man," Riah said, walking up in Roxy's face.

"I'm still your mother, and you will not disrespect me by cursing. Do I say shit 'bout you flossing around with Fizz? You have somebody. Don't you think I get lonely too? Your father isn't here. I won't be miserable for the rest of my life," Roxy said, standing toe to toe with Riah.

I saw the look in Riah's eyes. I guess Fizz did also, because he was walking over to Riah.

"Come on, y'all. This shit ain't about to happen. Y'all are family. Dozer and I will handle this shit in the streets. If y'all want to go to Augusta, then maybe it's best until this shit is over and done with," he said.

"Yeah, it is best we do," Kiya chimed in.

We talked a bit more. Kiya was really pissing me off. She was ride a die before. Now she's so pressed to leave a nigga, but on the real, she was a distraction at the moment for me. I needed to clear my head so we could handle these niggas.

I looked down at my phone, and it was my mom calling. Being single was probably not a bad idea for me. I was so busy trying to get Kiya together, I forgot we sent that nigga to our mom's.

"Shit, Fizz! We got to go. This mom calling," I said.

"Mom?" Nikki asked, standing in the doorway.

"Yes, we needed her to fix someone up so that we can holla at them. Now Nikki... don't start tripping. You already know how we get down. We out though, so come lock up."

I looked at Kiya, and she wouldn't even look at me. I walked out the house, and Fizz was right behind me. Riah called his name, but he told her he had to go. It was going to be a long night for us. That's for sure.

"Okay, bro. Where to, first?" Fizz asked.

"Shit... Chris and Ant can wait. The longer it takes, the scarier they'll be. Let's go see if mom can fix that nigga up enough to talk," I said.

"Cool, man. We hadn't had any problems like this since Naz went away."

"Man, I was thinking the same thing."

"So what's up with Kiya?" he asked.

"Man, I'm not sure. I think I should give her some space though."

"Like break up space?" he asked,

"Shit, man. I don't know, but anyway, you ain't got nothing on Arielle yet?" I asked.

"Hell nah. She ain't called that phone Mason had. Matter of fact no, one has called. Maybe this was his phone he talked with his brothers and Chris on, because Nikki's number isn't in here nor are any messages from her to him. She mentioned they text all the time. No pictures or nothing."

"That's suspicious. That's how they probably tracked us, if that's even Mason's brother," I said.

We talked more about the shit that happen and our plan while he headed toward our mom's crib. I heard my stomach growl again. I remembered I hadn't eaten shit that whole day. I knew I would get sick messing with Killa and Fizz. Those niggas always did some raw and uncut shit to nigga's bodies they were torturing. I was one that would put a bullet in their head and get it over with. I looked over at my brother and wondered if he ever thought about being completely done with this shit. I was just about to ask him when my phone rang.

"What's up, mom?" I asked her.

"Don't 'what's up, mom' me! You sent this burnt muthafucker over here. Killa talking about fix him up. What the fuck I look like… a damn ER? Y'all better be on your way here… got me cursing and shit. Lord, I tell you. Tell Fizz to wipe that silly looking smirk off his face, because ain't shit funny," she snapped.

I hung up and looked at Fizz. Our mom didn't play that shit, talking about sending that burnt muthafucker over there. I tried so hard to hold my laugh in.

"Man, how she knew I was smiling?" Fizz asked.

"Nigga, because you always laughing when she cursing me out, but when she curse your ass out, you don't be laughing then," I laughed.

We made it to our mom's, and she was working on the nigga that Killa put in his trunk. His ass was burnt. I thought about him being in Killa's trunk. It probably didn't help the situation either.

Our mom came out the room while Killa stood in there, watching over the burnt man.

"So you guys put the man in the trunk? Y'all lucky he didn't die. He's not going to make it though, so y'all better get the shit over with and get his burnt ass out of my house. I did the best I could with him. The burns are just too bad," she said.

Fizz and I walked into the room. Killa had this look on his face like he wanted to laugh, but he dared not until we left. Our mom would kick all of our asses.

"Did you get anything out of him," I asked Killa.

"Yeah, he say they call him OG."

"OG... so you're Mason's brother?" I asked.

He answered yeah. I wasn't expecting for him to sound like Freddy Krueger and shit. I knew he probably would have had a hard time talking, but damn.

"So what y'all thought... you could come here and take over? Well, now look at you... burnt up and shit," Fizz laughed.

"Is Mason dead?" he asked in that Kruger voice.

"Yes, he is, but how many of you were in the truck?" I asked.

"It was my two brothers, two of my homies, and myself. Please take me out of my misery. Please just kill me," he said with his voice fading out.

We asked him a few more questions, trying to get a feel of those northern niggas. One thing I knew was they were known to fold. He knew he was going to die, so he just told everything. Us southern niggas would've taken that shit to the grave. He said he didn't have a family. He only had his brothers. Their parents died years ago. He mentioned a girl's name. She was Mason's girlfriend. I mentally stored that name in my head. Not only was he a snake, but he played Nikki's ass. That's for sure.

We called the cleanup crew, and they did what they needed to. OG served his purpose. Now, he could join his brothers in hell. We talked and apologized to our mom, and she said if we did Sunday dinner at her house with our ladies, she would forgive us. I didn't even know if I would still have a girl after this shit, but I promised her we would.

We headed toward the warehouse. It was time to put in work. Once we made it in, we got suited and booted. Once we got ready, Killa brought out all of the tools for Fizz. Ant's eyes grew wide, and he started crying out, saying he was sorry. Chris had his head hanging low. Fizz walked right up to him and stood in front of him.

I walked right up to Chris as he sat there tied up with his head hanging low. I wanted him to hear my voice, so he knew I was still alive.

"So you thought taking my girl was going to make you rich?" I said. He raised his head up quick as if he saw a fucking ghost.

"Yeah, bitch. I'm alive, so you didn't think you were going to get caught? Well, fucking with a Boss like me, you should've known better.

"Man, look. I didn't have a choice. Mason said if I—"

"Don't insult me like that. Be a man about the shit. You did what you did. Now, how you die should be what's relevant," I said as I looked him straight in the eyes. I wanted to get this shit over with, because it was becoming hot as hell in the warehouse.

I glanced over at Ant. He was sweating bullets. I laughed at him. He wanted to be the man so bad that he didn't take the time to see how my brother and I built this shit up from the ground. As much as I did for his ass, he should've been working for free. I walked over to him. He knew I didn't tolerate disloyal ass niggas in my crew, so he knew he had to go.

"Ant, you know what pisses me off the most? It is that you thought giving me a little information would get you off the hook."

"Fizz, fuck you. You think you're some God, when you're just like the rest of us niggas. You're going to kill me anyway, so I might as well tell you how the fuck I feel," he said.

"That's your biggest problem, my nigga. You talk too damn much. For the record, I will never be like you two snake ass niggas. I'm a Boss, and if that makes me seem like a God, then nigga, I'm your God," I said, as I raised my gun up to his head. Dozer, Killa, and Sir all raised their guns at Ant's head. It was our signature for killing any snakes we found in our crew.

"Yo, who gon' read him his discharge rights?" I asked.

"Shit, I will. You've been caught by a boss," Killa said. We started shooting until his head was practically off his shoulders.

The look on Chris's face was priceless. There's nothing more thrilling then getting ready to kill someone who acted so tough and watching them bitch up. I was contemplating what I wanted to do with Chris. I wanted to do something I'd never done before. I had all of my soldiers in the warehouse. They all stood at attention, waiting for a chance to kill.

I walked toward Chris. I could smell the fear on him. I turned to my team.

"I need a moment of silence, please. I need to visualize how I want him to die."

While everyone was silent, I started thinking of how I could cut all his fingers off…the same fingers he grabbed Riah with. Then, I heard a noise. It sounded like someone was walking. The sound was unusual for our warehouse, because it sounded like a woman's heels clicking against the floors. As whoever it was got closer, I heard a second set of clicks, meaning there were two people. My crew all had their guns out and ready.

"Well, I can honestly say I've never had the pleasure of having men so quiet once I've entered the room," Nikki said as she walked in, dressed in an all-black jumpsuit with some heels on.

"Have you, Diva?" Nikki asked, and De'Kiya walked closer, making her presence known.

"No, I can't say that I have," she said. She was also dressed in all black. I thought that shit was sexy as fuck, so I knew Dozer was over there drooling at the mouth.

I didn't say anything. I just let them do whatever they came to do. I knew Nikki's hardheaded ass wouldn't stay away for long.

"Well, hello, Chris. It seems as if you have something I need," Kiya said, walking closer to him. Dozer walked up behind her. I knew he wanted to stop her, but she came this far, so there was no turning back.

"When a Queen speaks, you answer. Speak back… say something," Nikki said to Chris.

"What do I have that you need?" he asked.

"Your life," Kiya said as she raised the gun she had in her hand at him. Dozer looked at her like she wasn't serious.

"Wait, sis. Let me read this fool his discharge rights. You've been caught by a boss bitch," Nikki said, as she raised her gun, and they both let off shots. Kiya's aim was on point. It went straight to his head.

"Damn, sexy. Come here," Dozer said, grabbing Kiya and tonguing her down. I knew he was feeling that shit. I wanted to do something different to that nigga. I guess I got my wish.

"What the hell? Did y'all just add 'bitch' to our discharge rights?" Killa asked, laughing.

"Sure did. Now, men… get to work. Clean this garbage up," Nikki voiced like a true boss. The men didn't hesitate to do what she asked.

As we started walking out, we took off the shit we were wearing. I asked about Riah. They said she was still at Dozer's house. Mina went home because her mom kept calling asking questions. I still can't believe that Roxy told them that shit about us. I had two people I still needed to find, but that could wait. I wanted to just be in my baby's arms tonight. Dozer and I asked what happen with them leaving for Augusta. Kiya said Nikki changed her mind, and she decided to stay.

Riah

I laid with Rico as he fell asleep. He didn't want me to leave his side, so I didn't. My mind wouldn't stop thinking. Fizz was out there doing God knows what to Chris. I tried calling him, but it went straight to voicemail. Nikki said they always turned their phones off when shit like that went down. We decided not to go to Augusta, thanks to Nikki. She talked a good game. I really did like her. My mom and I didn't really talk. She went her way, and I went mine. I hoped she wasn't back on drugs, because I wouldn't hesitate to take my brother away from her! I started thinking about Fizz when my phone rang. My phone was in Fizz's car when I got kidnapped. I was happy Nikki got it for me. I answered, and it was Mina.

"Riah, I have someone on the line who wants to talk to you," she said.

"Hello? I asked, wondering who it was.

"Riah, it's me… Mo," he said.

"Nigga, you've got some nerve, trying to contact me."

"Riah, please let me explain. I swear I'll be honest."

"Where are you?" I asked.

"I'm at home. Please just give me ten minutes," he pleaded.

"You got two minutes, and I'm hanging up!"

"Riah, when Chris asked me to help him pull a prank on you,

45

I thought it was just that… a prank. So once I found out he was legit trying to hold you for ransom, I tried to stop him. He pulled a gun on me and told me to keep my mouth shut. I didn't want to be involved with that shit, so I just left."

"Yes, you fucking left me. Who knows what could've happen to me if Fizz wouldn't have found me."

"Fizz? He's alive?" he asked.

"Nigga, what… you thought he wasn't? Yes, my man is alive, and he's going to kill you."

"Riah, you have to believe me. I didn't want it to turn out like it did. I'm so sorry."

"Sorry… you're sorry? You can't be serious right now. Mina, please hang up on him."

She did just that.

"Riah, do you think he could be telling the truth?' she asked.

"I don't know. Even if I did, Fizz isn't going for that."

"I know, and that's why you can stop him. I hate he played a part in it to begin with, but I honestly think he was telling the truth. I'm sure he was scared and didn't know what to do. Chris is crazy."

"What am I supposed to tell Fizz? Baby, even though he helped Chris try to kidnap me, he thought it was a joke, so please don't hurt him?"

"Riah, the shit with Chris was foul. After all that shit he did to you and him putting his hands on me, he deserved to die."

"He was hitting you, Mina?" I asked.

46

"Yes… first, it was only a few times, and then it started happening all the time."

"Wow, Mina. Why didn't you say anything?"

"Because I was afraid of him. He pulled a gun on me before too. He said he was playing, but I think he was serious."

"What? OMG, I think Fizz and them are back. I'll call you back tomorrow with details," I expressed.

"Okay, and Riah… I love you."

"I love you, too. Oh, and Mina… do you think your mom would say anything about what happened?" I asked.

"No, my mom actually knows their lawyer. They are good friends. She said for you guys to just be careful, and to make sure you know what you are dealing with."

"Wow, but are you sure you're okay? This has to be hard for you?" I asked, wondering how she kept it all together. Shit, I don't know how any of us are keeping it together, knowing somebody you're involved with kills. That shit was so sexy, though. I felt a tingle between my legs.

I got off the phone and got out of the bed with my brother to go find everyone. Once I made it to the living room, I saw him, and he was looking so sexy. My man was dangerous, and I loved it.

"Come here, baby," he said, calling for me to come to him. I hugged him tightly, and he hugged me back. He whispered in my ear that the worst part was over. I can tell he had the weight of the world on his shoulders.

"You okay? I asked.

"Yes, now that I'm in your arms."

"You hungry?"

"Hell yeah! What you cook?" Dozer asked, jumping in the conversation. We all laughed. I told him what Roxy cooked and that it was on his stove.

Fizz pulled his phone out to call someone named Francine about a house as we sat down on the couch. She wasn't real happy he called so late, but she assured him she would have something for him tomorrow.

I asked if his ear still hurt, and he said a little. I wanted to make him feel better. Deedee left the room. I'm not sure exactly where she went, but she didn't say too much to Dozer or any of us.

After a while, Fizz told everyone we were about to retire to bed. I was happy, because I was exhausted. He showered, came back out, and laid on the bed on his stomach. He seemed stressed. I asked if I could help relax him.

"Sure," he said. I climbed on his back and rubbed his shoulders. I added a bit of pressure, and he said that it felt so good.

"How is your ear?" I asked.

"It's straight. In a day or two, the pain will completely be gone, and my mom put some type of medicine on it, so it's numb right now."

He closed his eyes and I whispered I love you in his ear. He smiled, showing those sexy dimples.

"I love you more, baby."

I kissed the back of his neck and slid my tongue along where I was kissing.

"You miss daddy?" he asked.

"Of course… it has been a minute," I said. He turned over. I sat on top of him, facing him. He kissed me, and I kissed him back. I couldn't wait to feel that feeling again. The pleasure he gave me was something I wished I could have forever.

"Take your clothes off," he instructed.

"Fizz, my mom is in the other room, and we have a house full of people," I said, but really wanting him to satisfy my needs.

"Really… you asked to relax me."

"That didn't mean sex."

"Okay, cool. Well, good night. I got shit to handle tomorrow."

I looked at him, pissed, like did he really just let me tell him no? He didn't even try to get some. I sat there, waiting to see if he would change his mind. When he didn't move, and I heard him snore, I got pissed and got up to go see who was up. Yeah, I was pissed, trying to be respectful of my mother and Dozer's house. I didn't even get any.

I walked into the living room, and Dozer was on the couch. I looked around, wondering where Deedee was. I looked at him, and he also looked stressed. I sat next to him. Usually, I wasn't so open to others, but he really showed me that he cared.

"Hey, bro. You okay?" I asked.

"What's up, sis? Yeah, I'm good. What about you?"

"I'm good. You look stressed like your brother," I laughed.

"Yeah, something light… nothing to worry your little pretty head about."

"You sure? You can talk to me if you need to. I'm a great listener."

I tried to make him feel comfortable to talk. He looked at me for a minute and looked over his shoulders, I guess making sure no one was listening.

"Your cousin bugging, man. She's pissed I left her when we came to find you. She wanted to be there. I couldn't have her tagging along. You never know what can go down. I know she wanted to be there for you, and did she tell you she pulled a gun on me?" he laughed.

"What? When?"

"When you got kidnapped, she thought Fizz and I had something to do with it."

"Shut up, Dozer. No she did not."

"Sis, I swear she did, but she's basically saying she need some time to get past all of this. At first, I was thinking the same, but I love her, and I want her in my life," he confessed.

"Aww, that's sweet. I'll talk with her. So how is Nikki doing? I couldn't imagine having to kill someone. How do you all do that and sleep at night?" I asked, not being funny, but really wanting to know.

"On some real shit, you have to think like it's either you or them, especially if a person is disloyal. It won't be long before they try to snake your ass over and over. It's not easy. As far as Chris and Mason, it had to be done. You do know that, right?"

"Yes, I know. Oh, I wanted to tell Fizz, but he fell asleep on me. Mina said her mom is good friends with y'all lawyer. I had asked if she thought her mom would say anything about what she knows about y'all."

"Damn, if she's good friends with my lawyer, she A1, then. Thanks for checking in on that for me, because it's been crossing my mind. That's why your ass out here. Fizz fell asleep on you," he laughed.

"Yeah, love your brother, but I don't think I'm the one for him. I'm just starting to learn myself and other things. Maybe he needs someone older," I said, looking down at the white rug underneath my feet.

"Nope, don't do that, Riah. I don't care who you're with. Always be confident in yourself. Always feel that you are too good for a person, and if they have you, then it's them who's lucky."

"You're going to make me cry, but I'm serious. I don't know if I'm woman enough for him."

"Stop it. My brother loves you. Trust me. He wouldn't do what he did if he didn't," he smiled.

"Yeah, I guess. I can't believe I missed graduation. I try not to think about it, but that was the happiest day for me. I woke up so blessed and look… I didn't even make it. My mom is really starting to make me think she's using again. Did you hear her say she has a new man?"

"Yeah, I heard that shit, but at the end of the day, sis, I'm going to be here for you and lil' man. Whatever y'all need, I got y'all. I know it's a hard pill to swallow, but you can't watch your mother's every move. You'll drive yourself crazy," he uttered.

"You're right, but my brother deserves to be her main priority. Dozer, can I ask you something about Fizz's ex, Arielle?" I asked him.

"What's that?"

"Why did she feel the need to help them do that to me? Did they have a serious relationship like that for her to want me out the way?"

"Yes… sort of, but when you're obsessed with someone in the sick way she is, there's no limit to what you'll do. You have nothing to worry about, Riah. Go get some sleep. Y'all going house shopping tomorrow, so be ready," he laughed.

"I guess, but I hope you and Deedee can work things out."

"Me too, sis. Thanks for the talk," he said as he hugged me.

I walked back into the room, and Fizz was still asleep. I grabbed my cell phone and had three messages from Mo. I wished he would just leave me alone. He needed to just lay low. I walked down the long hallway until I found the room my mother was in. I heard her whispering.

"Oh yes, baby. I can't wait, either. I will be home tomorrow. I just had to take care of some things with my children… Yes, of course. You'll have to meet Riah. She is a little firecracker... Well, it's the weekend. What do you have in mind? I don't have to work until Monday… Great! I'll see you first thing tomorrow, or later today, I should say."

She hung up, and I pushed the door opened.

"Going somewhere?" I asked.

"Hey, baby. How are you doing?" she asked.

"I'm doing okay," I said, trying to hold back the tears.

"Come here, baby. I know that look better than anyone. Baby, mama is not doing drugs. Now, I am smoking a little weed, but that

52

just helps keep me calm. Riah, I know you were looking forward to graduation, and I am so sorry you didn't get a chance to make it. I don't want you to think about what you lost. Think of everything you have gained. You're going to culinary school. I'm so proud of you. You and Rico mean so much to me. I know I'm not the world's best mother, but this new guy I met is really nice, and he makes me happy. He actually doesn't like me smoking or drinking, but you know how hardheaded I can get. Baby, I'm not trying to go back. I'm working. I have a nice spot that I can raise Rico up," she said, all of that while rocking me back and forth like she used to. I felt so loved by her, and I needed that. There's nothing like a mother's love that can make your whole world better.

"Mom, I'm just so scared that I don't know what life has in store for me next. I'm so scared to be on my own without you and Rico," I confessed to her.

"Baby, you will do fine. Fizz may be a little more than crazy, but I have no doubt in my mind that he wouldn't do right by you."

"He wants me to move with him, I do love him, but I don't think I'm ready to play house," I said.

"Honey, you don't play house with a man like that. If you're not ready, then tell him that. If he's a real man, he may argue with you about it, but he'll respect it," she told me as she wiped my tears from my face.

"Mom, you have this twisted way of getting through to me."

"I'm not sure if that's a compliment or not," she laughed.

"It is," I laughed back.

We talked a bit more, and it was already starting to become light outside. She was moving the rest of her things into her new house. It wasn't nearly as nice as Dozer's home. You could probably fit her house inside of his, but it was exactly what she needed.

I left her room and walked back toward the room Fizz and I were occupying. I walked past a room, and I heard low cries. I stopped and put my ear to the door. I knew it wasn't Deedee, because I could tell her cry from anywhere. I gently twisted the knob and peeked in. I couldn't believe it was Nikki crying. I didn't want to make it seem like I was eavesdropping, but I hated to see her like that. I pushed the door open more and walked toward her, lying across the bed with her face in the pillow.

"Nikki, you okay?" I asked.

"Riah, is everything okay? Why aren't you sleeping?" she asked.

"Nikki, what's wrong?"

She looked at me, and I knew something was wrong. I saw pain in her eyes.

Nikki

I try to be so brave and hardcore around my brothers, but in the end, I'm still a woman. I'm a woman that can't seem to find love. I came into one of Dozer's bedrooms to rest, when I found myself crying. Mason really hurt me with the shit he did. He had me thinking he was really the one. How could I trust anyone after that shit? I started crying, trying not to let it all out. When Riah walked in and asked if I was okay, I asked why was she still up, trying to turn the attention back at her, but she didn't give up.

"I couldn't sleep, and your brother wouldn't hump on me after I told him my mother was in the house. He went to sleep. He didn't even try to get none after that," she said, looking at me with her arms folded across her chest. We both started cracking up. Her crazy ass always brought this amazing presence when she came around.

"Riah, I'm good. It's just Mason really had me fooled. I really gave him my heart, and all that time, he was using me to get at my brothers."

"You know, I don't know much about relationships, but what I do know is that you are human, Nikki. It's okay to cry and feel hurt. You don't always have to pretend like everything is fine. You are an amazing person. I'm sure there is someone out there that would love to have a woman like you," she said, smiling her beautiful smile. Melting my heart, my new little sister was just what I needed right now. I vented my heart out to her. She was someone that knew pain all too well and still managed to try and make other smiles. I started to tell her about Nazir. I even showed her pictures. She thought he was sexy, also. She told me not to tell Fizz she said that. We talked a little bit more, and I decided I needed to go. There was no use lying around when I had heads to do and a house to clear out. I needed to get rid of all of Mason's things.

I hugged Riah and took care of my hygiene until I could make it home and soak in my bathtub. I told everyone I was leaving, and I saw that De'Kiya was leaving as well. I noticed the tension between her and Dozer, and I wondered what had happened between them last night.

"Well… long night, I see," I said, looking between the two of them.

"Yeah, very long. This the first time I saw her since we tried to talk last night. Did she mention that she broke up with me?" Dozer asked. I didn't want to get in their business, but I knew he said that so I could talk to her.

"No, she didn't. Just give her time, Dozer."

"Give her time? I have to give her time to completely breakup with me? Nah, I'm not pressed about keeping a bitch that doesn't want to be kept," he stressed.

"Dozer, don't do that—" I was going to say, but Kiya walked right up to him.

"Bitch? No, you the bitch. I said we needed time to figure things out. You took it as me breaking up with you, but since I'm a bitch and all, it can be."

She walked out of the house, and Roxy came walking out with Rico.

"What's going on, Deedee?" she asked.

"I'm leaving. You can stay, but I need to get home," Kiya said.

"No, we are leaving also. Dozer, thanks for everything and your hospitality. I'll talk to her," she whispered as she headed out.

Once they left, I looked at Dozer. He had a temper that he needed to learn to control. Calling Kiya a bitch was wrong, even though I knew he was using it as a figure of speech. People didn't understand us, so saying that pissed her off.

"Bro, really? That's how you moving now?" I asked him.

"Man, you know I wasn't trying to call her a bitch. That's just how I talk, but I'm not about to keep chasing her ass."

"She's just scared. She did just kill someone."

"Which is exactly why I told her monkey ass to stay here to begin with," he stated.

"I don't think that is really bothering her, to be honest. I think... well I know it's because you didn't let her in on it at first. She really wanted to be there when y'all found Riah," I confessed to him.

"Okay, she could've just told me that. Instead, she wants space. I don't understand y'all women."

"Look just give her time, but don't give up on her. She loves you, and that scares her. She's not used to anyone being there for her family. That's something new to her."

"I'll try, but I'm serious about not chasing..."

"What? What's wrong with you?" I asked wondering why he paused.

"Your mama wanted all of us to come over for dinner, and I kind of owe her that."

"What? Why would you tell her that if you knew it wasn't going happen?"

"It's going to happen. I'll make sure of that," he said, smirking like something was funny.

"When is this dinner happening?" I asked.

"Sunday, so that I can at least convince Kiya to do that for mom."

"Yeah… okay, mister 'I ain't chasing no bitch'. You know you want that girl. Quit playing yourself."

"Man, shut up. Fizz's ass still sleep. Ain't he supposed to be looking for a house today?"

"Nigga, I'm about to go handle that now," Fizz said, walking out with Riah behind him. They were so cute together.

"Y'all be safe out here, and hit me up later. We still have business to attend to," Dozer said.

"I got you. I won't be long. You know Francine knows my style, so I guarantee the first house she shows me is going to be my new home," he said.

"Well, brother, it was nice doing business with you," I said, hugging him and still feeling bad about his ear.

"Yeah, sis. Riah said she coming to the shop tomorrow to get a touchup. They fucked my baby head up," Fizz laughed.

"Yeah, I was looking at that, but I didn't want to say anything, because it wasn't relevant at the time," I said as I smiled at Riah.

"Well, I'll see you then," Riah said, hugging me. I walked out with them because I had shit to do myself.

I made it home, ran my bath water, and turned my music on low. I had my peeps come change my locks. Even though Mason was dead, I knew I needed to be on point at all times. I slipped up once, and that shit wasn't happening again. I acted so foolish over that man. I should have known, but love got in the way.

I honestly thought he loved me. He just wanted my brothers, so I was the bait to get them. He wasn't attracted to me at all. When he came up to me at the club he had a whole mission planned out. I gave him my loving and he tried to kill my brother. I heard my phone vibrating against my table, breaking me of my thoughts. I lay my head against the tub and closed my eyes. I was going to get all of Mason's things out my house, because I was not about to come home later and still see them. I cleansed myself and got out the tub. I heard my phone vibrating again, but I ignored it. It was probably one of my clients, anyway.

After I lotioned down, I put on some jeans and a graphic tee-shirt that said "I slay heads for a living". I started collecting all of Mason's things. I walked into my walk-in closet and grabbed his duffle bag. I sat the stuff on my bed and opened the bag. When I opened it and reached inside, I wasn't expecting to see what I saw. It was full of money and an envelope with my name on it. I opened it and read it...

Nikki if you are reading this letter, it is because I am dead. Yes, I knew there was a chance that I could die trying to kill your brother, so I guess he won. I just want to first apologize, even though it doesn't matter now, but I did what I had to for my family. I came down here to take over, and I guess things ended badly. I'll be honest. At first, my goal was to get you to fall for me and get inside your head so that I could get to your brothers. First, it was Dozer who I was out to get, but Fizz was my biggest threat. I know this all sound crazy, and if I was still alive, trust me... this letter would have never been found. My goal worked, but I never thought that falling in love with you would be included in it.

You are a wonderful woman, and I did love you all of you. Please forgive me. I know my brothers probably would make their way there if they hadn't already, but watch out for them, I wouldn't want anything to happen to you after this war I started. Please, warn your brothers about them also. The money is for you, it's should be over $600,000. No one knew about the money except for me. Nikki, baby... I did love you, and I hope you can live on knowing that. I also want you to wear this ring I got. It's shaped in a heart. Thanks for giving me your heart.

Love always,

Mason, your man.

Remember I said that in the beginning when we met that I was your man?

Once I finished reading, the paper was wet. I cried at the first sentence. This shit was crazy. He really loved me, even though I believed him. My brothers came first. That's why I didn't blink nor hesitate to shoot him. He left money for me, why? I didn't need it, but I wasn't a fool. I would most definitely get it checked out first, and if it was legit, I was sure going to put it away. I didn't need it, but what was I going to do with it if I didn't want it... give it away? I think not. My phone vibrated again, bringing me out of my thoughts. I looked to see who it was, and it was Nazir calling from prison. I was stuck, trying to decide if I should answer or not. I decided I had no reason not to answer, so I did.

"Hello!"

I waited for the automatic recording to finish talking, so I could accept the call.

"Hello!" I said again.

"Damn, it's like that? I've been calling and writing and ain't heard from you. What's up with that?" he asked.

"Nazir, I've just been busy."

"Nikki, we better than that. Did Fizz tell you my time got extended two more weeks?" he asked. Shit, so much was going on, I couldn't remember if he did or not.

"Yeah, he did, but what's up? How you been?" I asked, trying to make small talk.

"Shit, I'll be good once I get the hell out of here."

"So you're still going to be on parole once you out, right?" I asked, curious to know where he was going to stay because he sold his house a few years ago.

"Hell nah. Once I leave from behind these gates, I'm done, baby."

"Oh okay, so where umm…where you staying?" I asked as I held my breath.

"Shit, I was hoping with you," he informed. I didn't know what to say. I didn't want to burst his bubble, but that wasn't happening.

"I'm just fucking with you, Nikki. I'm staying with Dozer until I buy another one. He said Francine already had a few lined up for me to see," he smirked. I exhaled after he said that.

"Oh, that's what's up," I said as I looked at the clock.

"I miss you though, Nikki, on some real shit. I know I told you to move on, but I—"

"Look, let's not do this, Nazir. What happened between us was in the past."

"So what… you don't love me anymore?" he asked. I hated when he did that. He knew damn well I'd always love him. He just liked to hear me say it.

"You'll always hold a place in my heart," I assured him.

"A place in your heart? Well I guess I'll let you go, and I'll see you when I'm out."

"Yep, hit me up," I said. We ended the call. I wondered if Dozer or Fizz told him about Mason. Probably not, because he most definitely would have mentioned it. I quickly put the money back in the closet along with the letter. I'd have my peeps come check it out later tonight. I gathered all of Mason's things and put them in a bag. I put the ring on my dresser, not sure what to do with it yet. Once I got outside, I threw his things into the trash.

Deedee

nce I made it home and got settled, I took a long bath. Roxy finished moving her things. She and Rico were at their new house getting settled in. My mind was all over the place with so many thoughts that I couldn't figure out which to tackle first. I wanted to cry, smile, pray, and sleep all at once. I wasn't thinking about that shit with Chris. He deserved what he got. Anyone who touched or harmed my family could get what he got. I'd have to deal with God later, but asking for forgiveness and what I did in the meantime.

After that shit went down and Dozer tried to keep me out the loop really pissed me off. When I did come in that bitch with all black and heels, he was turned on by it. Either way, I think him and I need to take things slow. I don't know if I was just so mad I couldn't get past it and see that I really loved him. Yeah, I was being stubborn. But him calling me a bitch just set it off for me. I called Riah and asked if she could come over after her and Fizz looked at houses, and she said she would. It was going to just be her and I.

I was sitting around watching TV when my doorbell rang. Riah still had a key, so I didn't think it was her. I got up to open the door, but peeped out the window first.

"Damn, he just had to bring his ass over here," I said to myself. I opened the door and walked away from it. I turned around, and he was just standing in the entrance of the door.

"Are you going to come in and shut my door?" I asked him.

"You never invited me in?" he said. Now his ass was picking with me. He brought his crazy ass over here without me telling him to.

"Dozer, you can come in," I said, not feeling the energy to play his game.

He walked in and hugged me. I knew this nigga had to be crazy for him to think shit was sweet. I pushed him away.

"So you call me a bitch, and now you're here hugging me? What's up with that?" I asked.

"I wasn't calling you a bitch directly, Kiya. It's just the way I talk, and how you took it."

I looked at him. This back and forth shit was becoming too much for me. We played the staring game for what seemed like forever.

"Kiya, I love you. You do know that, right?" he asked.

"Dozer, why did you sneak off and leave me? I told you I wanted to be there when you found Riah?"

"Kiya, is that why you're tripping, because I didn't want you in harm's way? That's what a man does for his woman. He protects her," he said, raising his voice a little.

"No, I can protect myself."

"Okay, this shit crazy. I'm sorry for trying to protect you, if that's what you want to hear."

"No, I want to hear you walk back out my house. Why did you even come here? You ain't say shit when your sister was down to ride, but you're tripping because I wanted to?"

"De'Kiya, what exactly are you mad at, because I'm confused?"

"Oh, so by you saying my whole name makes you serious?" I said picking with him.

"You are so fucking childish. Please just tell me what you're really mad at?"

"Dozer, it's clear we are not on the same page. Riah is my family, and I wanted to be there for her."

"Okay, you don't think she knows that? Why are you making it such a big deal? She's over the shit and it happened to her move on, before you lose something you'll regret," he said.

"Lose something I'll regret? What, you? Well, if that's how you feel, you can just leave."

"Kiya, please. I came here because I want you in my life, and also that I told my mother that I would bring you over for Sunday dinner," he confessed.

"I know you did not lie to your mother, did you?" I asked.

"No, I didn't lie, because you're going to be there. I can't disappoint her like that. Please just do that for me. Riah will be there with Fizz, so it will be all of us."

"You are something different. You know that?" I mentioned.

"Well, you think I'm sexy, don't you?" he asked, coming close to me.

"No, not really, I'll see you at your moms Sunday," I said, backing up.

"Sunday? Damn, that's the only day you plan to see me?"

"Yep."

"Are you serious, you do realize you are acting childish, and for what?"

"Look, we are very different. I'm independent and don't like people trying to decide what's good or bad for me."

"So this whole thing about me leaving you at my house because I wanted to protect you got you feeling like that? So, the shit that went down with Chris hasn't crossed your mind?

"Yes, it does, and yes, it crossed my mind. I'm not some serial killer that likes doing it, but I knew it had to be done. Honestly, I think I could do it again if I had to."

He just stared at me, and I had to turn away. I wonder how long he was going to play the staring game with me until I caught him staring me down.

"What are you looking at?"

"Your mean sexy ass," he smiled, showing that dimple.

"Bye, Dozer."

He didn't say anything, but he shook his head on the way to the door. Maybe I was trying to purposely push him away. I don't know why, though. I didn't sleep at all at his house, mainly because I was mad at him the whole time. I went to my bedroom and laid across my bed. I put my phone on vibrate and tried to turn my brain off.

I felt someone shaking me, and I heard them say wake up. I looked up, and it was Riah. She was glowing and smiling. Here I was, stressing about what happened to her, and she was living like she didn't have a care in the world. I smiled at her and got up.

"Let me brush my teeth, and then I want to hear all about this house that you and Fizz got," I said, walking into my bathroom.

"Mom called me. She said she was pretty much settled in her house. Rico seemed happy too when I talked with him.

"Oh yeah?" I said as I came out the bathroom. We went into the living room and sat on the couch. I grabbed some wine from the fridge and a wine glass and sat down.

"Want some?" I asked her.

"No, I have to drive my car back to our home later. We picked out furniture, appliances, and wall décor. Francine is really nice and good at what she does. He saw the first house and didn't want to look any further at the others."

"Okay, I see y'all," I said, eyeing her.

"Well, there is one problem that I didn't mention to him yet."

"What's that?"

"I didn't tell him I wasn't going to actually be staying there like permanently... at least, not yet."

"Really, Ray? That probably should have been the first thing you said to him."

"I know. I plan to tell him tonight, but I saw how big the bed is. I don't want him to put me out after I do. I just want to lay in the bed first," she laughed.

"Good luck with that. So, are you going to stay here?" I asked, hoping she would.

"Actually, no. I'm in the accelerated culinary program, so free housing comes with that. I have to go look at the place Monday. They're apartments, and I will have a roommate, but I just want to be on my own first?"

"Yes, I get that. Well, do what makes you happy," I stated.

"Can I ask how did it go with Chris? Did you see him get killed?" she asked.

"Nope, he was a dead man before I got there. How are you feeling about all of this?" I asked her.

"Well, I've never known anyone personally that killed someone, but the reason behind it, I get. I'm not scared or anything. I actually feel safe around Fizz. Oh, OMG! I forgot to tell you. Mo called me," she said as if it was nothing.

"What? Did you tell Fizz and Dozer?" I asked.

"No, because he explained what happened, and I honestly think that he was telling the truth."

I couldn't believe she still didn't tell Fizz. She told me the story, and he could have very well been somewhat innocent in all of this, especially if he was at home like he didn't have a care in the world.

"One other thing, Deedee. Fizz said he is going to buy me a car. I told him it's a waste of money because you already bought me one. He said 'my girl' ain't going to keep driving around in a 2000 Honda Accord, and her man driving a fucking Lamborghini, Bentley, and a Porsche. I told him to give me one of them. This fool said 'nah, those are my babies. I'll get you something else'," she said, laughing and mocking him. I laughed just as hard.

"OMG, Fizz is out of his mind, but whatever you want to do with your car, do it. It's yours."

"So you're not mad? I mean, you did buy it."

"No, I'm not mad. Shit, tell him to tell his brother to get on the car buying bandwagon."

I laughed. We talked a bit more about everything, our feelings for these brothers, Roxy, Mina, and just life. She finally gave in and told me she had been letting Fizz hit it, like I didn't already know. She stayed for a bit longer and finally left. I walked her to her car and hugged her tightly. She called and talked to me the whole way to their new home, even though she didn't want to live with the man. I couldn't wait to see it. It took her about forty-five minutes to get there.

It was really quiet tonight. Usually, I'd hear the kids down the street, arguing about who can play ball better. I pulled out my phone and looked up Dozer's name. I wanted to call him, but didn't. Instead, I called Nikki and asked if she wanted to go out for dinner and drinks. I was happy she took me up on my offer.

My ear was actually feeling better. I took the dressing off and changed it. It actually didn't look bad, so I kept it off. My mom was a great nurse. She asked how it was doing, and I told her good. I thanked her for caring for me.

When I dropped Riah off to her car, I was happy to get her away for a minute. Killa called, and they spotted Arielle. She still had yet to text or call Mason's phone, so I texted her to see what I could get her to say.

Me: You good to go.

Arielle: Damn! I was starting to think y'all fucked some shit up. I'm in town. Can I get my man now, or is that bitch still in my house?

Me: Nope, she's dead, but I want to give you your cut. Where are you?

Arielle: I told you that I don't need your money. As a matter of fact, I can get you right, if you know what I mean?

Me: Yeah, you can do that for me. I'm sending the address where I want you to meet me right now.

Arielle: Okay, got it. On my way now. I can't WAIT to taste you.

She had to be the dumbest bitch alive. She was going to be meeting her maker. I didn't have time to play with her ass. I told Killa to handle her, and let me know when she was dead. Riah had texted, saying she was on her way, so my focus was on her. I was already trying to get the house settled. All the movers in the world still couldn't move fast enough for me. I was very impatient with stuff like that. Maria was working overtime, trying to at least make it comfortable enough for us to get a good night's sleep.

After I got off the phone with Dozer, letting him know Arielle was taken care of, Riah was pulling in. Maria had just finished our bedroom, and I was beyond tired. *With everything going on, I didn't get a chance to tell everyone about having a mini graduation for Riah. I needed to put something together for my baby.* She walked, in ending my thoughts about it.

"Hey, baby," I said, meeting her at the door.

"Hey, I'm hungry. I can whip us something up real quick," she said.

"Yeah gon' head and do that. You haven't cooked for me yet," I smiled, watching her head into our kitchen. As I watched her move around like she owned it, I knew she would make a great chef.

"So you think your nachos are going to be the best I ever had?" I asked, watching her add her special touch.

"Why of course, but I won't brag about it. I'll let your mouth tell me what you think."

"I can't wait to taste you later on," I said, biting my lips.

"What you say?"

"Nothing, hurry up. I'm hungry."

"Don't rush me. You can't rush great taste. Remember that," she laughed.

About twenty minutes later, we were sitting at the island, eating. I couldn't even tell her how good it was, because I stuffing my face. Shit was fye as hell, and I couldn't wait to get seconds. She finished eating, cleaned her plate, and I finally looked up and told her that it was delicious.

"You want some more?" she asked.

"Not right now. Right now, I want some of you," I said, walking toward her.

"Oh yeah? Come get me."

I pulled her to the steps heading to our bedroom. With every step, I took advantage and grabbed her ass and breast. She turned around and pecked me on the lips. We made it to the bedroom, and I pushed her to the bed. I gripped her breast, pulled her shirt and bra off, and immediately started sucking her nipples. She reached down and started caressing my dick. It was already hard. Now, my shit was even harder. She pulled down my pants, and I took off her pants and panties. She began moving her hand up and down my dick. I inserted two fingers inside of her dripping pussy. Her shit was gripping the hell out of my fingers. I couldn't wait to stick my dick in her. I started playing with her, making her moan.

"Umm hmm… yeah," she moaned.

"You like that shit, don't you?" I asked.

"Yes… Umm! Please give me the dick," she gasped.

I pulled my dick out and inserted it in her tunnel. It was so wet and tight. I didn't have on a condom when I knew I should have. I started deep stroking, making her moan even louder. My phone vibrated, and it was my brother. I had to answer it because of all the shit that's been going on. I had to make sure he was straight.

"Yo!" I said, breathing hard.

"Umm, Fizz! Go harder," she said, and I knew Dozer heard her.

"Damn! Y'all over there fucking? I was just hitting you up. Guess I'll call you tomorrow," he said, and I can tell he was smiling.

"Damn, yeah bro. Get at me tomorrow."

I hung up and started pounding harder. She was damn near screaming now.

"Yes… umm hmm. I'm cumming, Fizz," she said as she gasped for air. She asked if she could suck it. I knew she wasn't experienced, but I didn't want to turn her down. I laid down on the bed facing her, and she gently wiped my dick off with her hand. She took my dick into her mouth. She played with the head for a second. I was hoping she didn't scrape my dick with her teeth. I wasn't sure if she knew what she was even doing. Next thing I know, she started slurping on my dick and moving her hands up and down my shit. She was swallowing my whole dick, making it disappear inside her mouth.

"Damn, Riah. This shit feels so good. Ahh shit! Just like that, baby…Damn, girl! Where the fuck you learn… ahh shit, yes. Damn, I'm about to bust."

When she started bobbing that head up and down, it was over. My toes started curling up. She swallowed every drop of cum. I had to get myself together. I wanted to still cum inside of her pussy, but there was something I had to get off my chest first.

"Riah, where the hell did you learn how to suck dick like that?" I asked, getting pissed.

"Calm down. I watched these porn videos online. I wanted to make sure I knew how to please you."

"Damn, I love you, girl," I said, as I tongued her down. I inserted my dick inside her pussy from the back. All I could think about was her giving my pussy away. I would body her and that nigga. I started pounding in and out, fast. She started moaning which was music to my ears.

"Damn, girl. This shit so good," I stated, grabbing her hair. She started throwing the pussy back at me.

"God damn...ahh, yeah! I'm about to cum, baby," I said.

"You like that, daddy, don't you?" she softly asked.

Riah's ass came two more times when it was said and done. I put her ass right to sleep. I was wide awake and wouldn't mind another round. I decided to let her be. I called Dozer back. I needed to tell him I was getting married. I had to lock that pussy down.

I walked down the stairs, letting my sleeping beauty sleep. I walked around the corner and saw Maria. Damn, I forgot she was even here. I knew she probably heard Riah... shit, even me moaning.

"What's up, Maria?" I asked.

"Fizz, I be done for the day. Just putting the rest of décor up in your basement, or you man cave. You like, right?"

"Yes, I love it Maria, but go ahead and go home. You did enough already."

"Okay, boss. You have nice girl. She is beautiful," she said. It always tripped me out how she talked.

"Thanks, Maria. I'll let you meet her since she's going to be the lady of the house. I'll see you Sunday at Mom's, right?"

"Yes, she makes dinner, and I can't wait to eat... I... I mean clean for her," she laughed.

"Yeah. Okay, Maria. I know you like her soul food," I said as I walked her to the door. I watched her get into her car and the gate open and shut. I called Dozer and talked to him for a bit.

After I hung up with Dozer, I was laughing at his ass. He was jealous that he wasn't getting any. He didn't even know if him and Kiya were together or not. Riah came down the stairs, and I couldn't stop staring at her. She was so beautiful.

"So you have been studying sex moves online and shit. What else you learn?" I teased her.

"I'd rather show you than tell you," she smiled.

"Yeah, okay," I said and smirked.

"What's up? You good?" I asked her.

"Yes, but I wanted to talk about something with you. I know you are going to get mad, but I have to express how I feel to you," she said. I was happy she felt that way. I wanted an open relationship where we could talk about anything.

"Okay, go ahead. I'm listening," I said, as I laid back on my couch, giving her my full attention. She seemed hesitant at first, but she finally started talking.

"Fizz, when I got accepted into the accelerated culinary program, housing was a part of that package, and I can get my own apartment. I will have a roommate, but you know…"

After she finished, I just stared at her. She was talking about a damn apartment like she wasn't living up in a damn mansion.

"Please say something. It's not like I don't want to live here. Who wouldn't? I just need to be independent and on my own, first. I mean, I'll spend the night some nights."

She was going on and on. All I heard was, basically, I don't want to live with you.

"Fizz?"

"What up?"

"Did you hear me?"

"Yes, I did."

"Okay, and what's your response?" she asked.

"Okay."

"Okay? What does that mean?"

"It means okay, Riah. You want to live on your own? Okay, cool."

"So you good with that?"

"Look… you mentioned this, not me. What is it exactly that you want me to say?"

"I'm not looking for a certain response. I just thought you would be more upset," she mentioned.

"Well, I sure ain't fucking happy about it, but that's what you want."

I didn't get her. At Dozer's house, she told me no about sex, then got mad that I didn't pressure her for it. Now, it seemed as if she wanted me to be mad that she decided to not live in the house I bought for us.

"Whatever, Fizz," she said.

"Wait… what do you want me to say, baby," I asked.

"Nothing… nothing at all."

I laughed at her. Yes, I was pissed, but why make a fuss about it? I didn't have cable set up yet, so watching her was very entertaining.

"So when do you move into the apartment, and when do you start your classes?" I asked.

"I have to go sign up for the apartment Monday, and the classes start in a few weeks."

"Okay, that's what's up. I'm proud of you. Come over here and lay with me."

She got off her couch and came to lay with me. She was a breath of fresh air for me. She wanted to be independent, so I was going to let her. We laid on the couch and talked for a minute. She brought up the Chris thing, and I knew Arielle was the next conversation coming up. I just told her the truth… that she was dead.

"Now, I just have to get Mo, and I can finally chill," I said, looking down at her as she laid flat on the couch while I was propped up.

"Fizz, I really don't think he had much to do with it."

"He had something to do with it. He helped Chris. That's something."

"Well, I just think we should just let him be," she commented.

I looked at her crazy. She didn't say that shit about Chris. What was so special about Mo?

"What? Why you defending him?"

"I'm not defending him. I just think he didn't play a major part in it."

"Is there something you want to tell me, Riah?" I asked.

"No, I was just stating what I felt."

"Well, when it comes to that nigga that helped kidnap you, keep those feelings to yourself. Now, excuse me while I go shower."

I damn near pushed her ass off the couch. I went upstairs, showered, and laid across my bed. I closed my eyes for what seemed like a second, but turns out it was longer.

Dozer

I was just leaving from my club. I was planning Naz a welcome home party. He was almost out that bitch. If he could've kept his cool, he would've already been home. I had about two hours before I needed to head to Sunday dinner with my mom. I was going to head over to De'Kiya's house, but I didn't have the energy to play her games. I called and texted her twice about coming to dinner today. She never responded back. However, she mentioned to Nikki she would be there.

This shit was crazy. She was acting childish. I'd been horny as fuck. A few of my old flames have been blowing my phone up, but I was trying to hold off until De'Kiya got her shit together. Shit, even if she did, we still weren't fucking. I had needs, and her ass was playing. Fuck around and have another woman on my arms, she was gon' be looking crazy.

I got home and called my mom. She was excited we were all coming over for dinner. She really loved that type of stuff. I was happy she was still living, because she was the rock that held us together. We talked while she was doing whatever she was doing. She sounded out of breath, and I told her to take it easy. Whatever wasn't done didn't need to be. She still had to take it easy. She had been doing so well. I remembered the long stay in the hospitals, and the long drives for treatments.

I got up so I could head over to my mom's house when my phone alerted me that I had a text message. It was Kenda. She sent a video of her pussy. She played with her ring down there for a minute, then she inserted her fingers, moving them in and out. I couldn't turn away, because my shit was hard as fuck. She was moaning, calling my name. I said fuck it, pulled my dick out, and started jacking my shit off. She pulled out a dildo and started sucking on it, saying that I tasted so good. She inserted it inside her pussy, bringing the camera closer. She pulled it in and out, continuously saying my name until she started cumming. I came right after she did.

"Damn, that shit felt good," I said to myself. I cleaned myself up before I had to head out. I opened the door smiling to myself that Kenda's little video did the job, even though I was going to curse the bitch out for sending that shit to my phone. Then again, shit... Kiya's ass wasn't sending me shit. As I looked up, I noticed Kiya's car pulling in.

I walked down the side walk, waiting to see what was up with her. My phone vibrated, and I prayed it wasn't Kenda ass. It wasn't, though. It was Nikki.

"What, sis?"

"Don't say it like I'm bothering you," she laughed.

"Man, what you want?" I said with a smirk.

"I'm at the shop. Swing by and get me before going to Mom's."

"How you know I haven't left yet?" I asked.

"Well, did you?"

"Man, bye. I'll be there in a minute. Why you can't drive your own damn car?"

"I'll be ready when you get here," she said as she hung up. I shook my head as Kiya walked toward me. She was looking sexy as hell. I wanted to just tongue her down, but who knew what type of mood she was in.

"Hey," she said all dry, with those plump lips drawing me in.

"What's good? I called and text you," I said, looking at how the sun was shining on her pretty face.

"Yeah, I know, but do you mind if we ride together," she asked.

"We can. I have to grab Nikki, too, so let's ride."

We drove in silence. I turned the radio on, and my shit, Usher's "No Limits", was playing. I started singing. Kiya looked over at me. I grabbed her hand and started singing to her.

"You better watch the road, before we crash," she laughed. I turned the radio down. I felt like it was the perfect opportunity to talk to her while she was smiling.

"On some real shit, Kiya, are we together or not? I need to know how to move," I said.

"How to move? What you mean?" she asked.

"I need to know if I should move on or not. You know how I feel about you, but I'm not about this chasing shit. I can have any chick I want, but I want you," I voiced.

"I really don't want to answer that right now, but let's just get through dinner with your mom. We can talk about it another time," she responded.

"So, you expect for me to just wait until you're ready? It don't work like that. What is wrong with you? If you tell me what the problem is, we can fix it," I vented. We had just pulled up to Nikki's shop.

"Can we just talk about this later? I don't like people in my business," she said.

"Who... Nikki? That's my damn sister! What the fuck you mean?" I asked.

"Can we just talk about this later?"

I didn't even answer her. I looked up and saw Kenda walking out with Nikki.

"Aww shit."

I didn't realize I had said that out loud, but I knew how messy Kenda could be. She walked toward the car with Nikki. I couldn't believe she had the audacity to be walking up to my shit

"Hey, Dozer. You enjoyed that video?" Kenda asked. I wanted to choke her ass for saying that.

"Kenda, stop sending that shit to my phone. That is disrespectful, on so many levels," I stated.

"Yeah... okay. Keep pretending for that thing over there," she said, looking over at Kiya.

"Bitch, do you have to show how thirsty you are?" Kiya asked. I knew some shit was about to pop off. I had never seen Kenda fight. I just heard her pop off at the mouth. I didn't feel like dealing with her shit today.

"Thirsty? Bitch, please! You don't think your man deleted the video, did you? I bet it's still in his phone," she articulated. I was starting to become very hot at that point. I didn't delete the video, which was irrelevant if I did or not.

"Kenda, why the fuck you starting shit? You need to go on before I get out this car. You being too damn messy right now," Nikki yelled.

"I'm not being messy, friend. You don't know your brother like I do. How long did it take for you to find out we were fucking?" Kenda asked.

"I'm 'bout tired of this bitch," Kiya said, getting out of the car... something I didn't want to happen. Nikki and I jumped out, also. I pushed Kenda back while Nikki tried holding Kiya back.

"Kiya, get back in the car. It's not worth it. You know she's being messy."

"Bitch, run up, and watch I drop your frog looking ass," Kenda said.

"Nikki, she don't know me like that to be making threats. Please, just let me get this bitch one time," Kiya said. Nikki let Kiya go and walked toward Kenda, so I hurried and grabbed Kiya.

"Baby, please let's just go. You're too pretty for all of this shit," I said, pulling her back to my car.

"You want to keep coming for my brother, now you got shit started. I told you, Kenda," Nikki said, trying to get a hold of Kenda.

"Nikki, I'll leave now, but he needs to stop lying," Kenda said, as she jumped into her car and drove off. She talked shit to Kiya, but was running from Nikki.

We got in the car and left. I knew this would start an argument, and I was right.

"So you still were fucking with that thirsty hoe?" Kiya asked.

"No, I'm not. She sent a video to my phone. That was the first time I heard from her," I said, being honest.

"Let me see the video!" she said.

"Kiya why would you want to see that shit," I expressed. I didn't want her watching it, knowing Kenda was moaning my name and shit.

"Let me see your phone, before I flip this car the fuck over."

I just tossed her the phone to give her what she wanted. I knew Nikki didn't like for chicks to be coming at me sideways no matter who they were.

She played the video and turned the volume up, loud as hell. I just focused on the road, waiting for what came next. Hearing Kenda call out my name again, I had to admit, my dick was starting to wake up again. This shit was unbelievable.

"Damn, Dozer. What the fuck?" Nikki asked.

"Man, that's your crazy ass friend. I put that shit on everything that I haven't fucked with that girl since Kiya and I been together," I confessed. I just hoped Kiya believed me. Now, I knew that we weren't going to be chilling together later on. If it wasn't one thing, it was another. Kiya tossed my phone back over to me and didn't say a word.

We made it to my mom's, and the car was silent as hell. I didn't even want to reach to turn the radio up, afraid that Kiya would snap. We got out the car. Fizz's car was there, so he and Riah must've already been inside.

We walked in and were welcomed with a wonderful smell. I couldn't wait to eat some fried chicken and cabbage. Fizz was in the kitchen, trying to steal food, as usual. I saw Riah and Mom talking. I could tell she was in awe of Riah.

"Hey, old lady," I said, hugging my mom.

"Boy, who you calling old?" she asked, hugging me back. She hugged Nikki and then Kiya. I pulled Fizz to the side so that I could tell him what went down. Kiya, Nikki, and Riah helped my mom in the kitchen.

"So Kiya was about to get in Kenda's ass? Man, you better nip that shit in the bud," he mentioned.

"Man, I am. The shit just seemed so crazy. One minute, I'm jacking off to the video, and next, she walking to my car," I said as I shook my head. We were talking and kicking it when Nikki walked in.

"Food ready!" she said and walked back out.

"Man, how is she really doing?" I asked.

"Shit, she say she good, bro. You know your sister shows no sign of weakness," he said as we headed to the dining room to eat.

My mom had a big ass table, but I knew she wouldn't approve of me sitting so far away. The seat that was left open for me was directly across from Kiya. Fizz sat next to Riah, which Kiya was on the other side of her. Nikki was next to my mom, and I was next to Nikki. My mom blessed the food, and we ate and had small talk. One thing about our mom was that she was blunt and funny as hell, so I hoped Kiya and

Riah didn't take whatever came out of her mouth offensively.

"Riah, I was watching you around the kitchen, and I can already tell your going to become a great chef. That's good, because that big-headed boy next to you loves to eat," my mom said.

"Thank you, Ms. Edgemen," Riah laughed.

"Call me Joyce, baby… or mom."

"Kiya, you're quiet. You okay?" my mom asked.

"Yes, I'm fine. The food is delicious."

I looked at Kiya. I knew she was mad at me, but this just justified what I was saying. She wanted space, but wanted to still act like we were in a relationship. After this, we were going to have a serious talk. I didn't want to pressure her, but damn. She was acting like a little ass kid.

"Thank you, baby. Make sure y'all take some to go," she said.

Riah and Fizz were all lovey-dovey. You couldn't help but smile at those two. I was happy she was holding up, though. He told us he wanted to plan her graduation ceremony with just us, her family, and Mina. I thought that was a good idea.

Mom got up and grabbed dessert while Maria cleared the table.

"Dang, she's like… everywhere," Riah said, looking at Maria.

"Yes, she's our housekeeper and maid," Fizz answered.

"She's the housekeeper and maid for all of y'all?" she asked.

"Yes, baby."

I could just imagine what she was thinking. One thing I liked about her and De'Kiya were that they weren't impressed by our money. That was really unusual for us.

My phone vibrated. I looked down, and it was Kenda's ass again. I looked up and Kiya was staring a hole in my head.

"What?" I asked. She just rolled her eyes, and it didn't go unnoticed by others at the table.

"What's wrong with you, Deedee?" Riah asked.

"Nothing... I'm good!"

"You sure, because that eye roll said differently," Riah pressed.

"Yeah, I'm good. Please excuse me. I have to use the restroom," Kiya stated.

She got up, and Riah looked over at me. I looked away, because I already told her how her cousin was acting the last time we chatted at my house. I deleted the message Kenda sent. She was starting to really piss me off. She was fucking up what I had going on with Kiya.

I looked through my messages and saw I had one I never read. I opened it, and it was a picture of the sexy chocolate chick. I never gave her my number, nor did I ever call her, so I wondered how she got my number. The picture she sent was of her sexy ass face. The message said "remember me". At the time, Kiya's grandma was in the stage of dying, and I thought we were going to actually have something by now. Otherwise, I would've never swerved her like that. Her name was Michelle, and she was throwing the pussy at me. Look at my ass now. I hadn't had any pussy in a while. I felt a presence behind me, so I looked up, and sure enough, my crazy ass sister behind me, looking all in my shit.

"Really, Nikki? Get your nosey ass on," I laughed.

"Yeah, we're going to talk later," she told me. She smirked as she walked off toward the kitchen.

"Tell mom I want ice cream with my pie while you in there," I yelled. Mom came back from the kitchen and sat down while Maria passed out our dessert.

"There is an alert on the news about a tornado watch. Maybe you all should stay here for the night," she said.

"We're gon' take that chance and go home. Otherwise, my baby going to be acting funny tonight," Fizz implied.

"Really, Fizz? That was so inappropriate," Riah said, looking embarrassed.

"Man, my mom knows what's up," he said with a smirk.

"Yeah, while you're sticking your little ass penis in her, you better be using protection. Don't mess her life up, boy. She has a good head on her shoulders," she said.

Man, I couldn't hold it in. I had to laugh. So did Nikki and Riah.

"Mom, I'm not a little boy anymore. Riah, tell her what I'm working with," he said, trying to defend himself.

"Boy, you're going to make me whoop your ass, talking like that at the table."

I laughed so hard. I dismissed myself to go see where Kiya was. She was missing all the action.

Deedee

I had to excuse myself from the table. I asked Joyce to show me the restroom. I called and checked on Roxy and Rico. They were watching movies. When I came to Dozer's house to ride with him to his mom's for dinner, I was trying to get over my little stubbornness. He was looking so good, coming out the house. That shit changed when we picked Nikki up. That bitch, Kenda, put his shit out there. Obviously, they had been still fucking around. Why else would the hoe send a video like that?

I used the restroom and washed my hands after. I put my hair up in a messy bun. I was feeling some kind of way after Dozer looked at his phone and had the nerve to be smiling. What the fuck had him smiling like that… another one of Kenda's videos? I wanted to jump over the table and slap his ass. I thought about it for a moment. I was acting kind of childish. I knew I couldn't play those games with him. Eventually, he would start messing with somebody else. I just felt like I needed to be single. I didn't know how to have a boyfriend, and I knew he had needs that I wasn't taking care of, so I guess that's where Kenda came into the picture. To keep from getting my heart broken, I think it's best I just ended it. Thinking about that, a tear came down my eyes. I needed to see Dr. Acres, because something was really wrong with me. I wiped my hand on the paper towel that I ripped off the roll and headed out the restroom. When I opened the door, Dozer was leaning on the wall and had scared the hell out of me.

"Dozer, you scared the shit out of me!" I said as I placed my hand on my chest. I came all the way out the bathroom and shut the door behind me. I thought that maybe he was waiting on the rest room, so I walked past him with no such luck. He grabbed me.

"You straight?" he asked.

"Yes... now, excuse me."

You could hear the high winds. I guess he noticed me looking around, because he said it's a tornado watch.

"I wasn't fucking with that girl, on everything," he said.

"I'm not tripping. That's y'all business, what y'all got going on."

"So why were you about to beat her ass?"

I didn't have a comeback for that one. I just switched my weight to one leg and stared at him. I self-consciously licked my lips as he stared back at me.

"Stop playing games, De'Kiya. That's not a good look for you."

He walked toward me and pushed me against the wall.

"I want you and only you. I'm not going to keep chasing you, though. You've got twenty-four hours to figure out what you want," he said as he kissed me. I kissed him back and his hands roamed my body, giving me that feeling again. I don't know why I was giving this man so much trouble, but until I figured that out, I had to end it.

"Dozer, I don't need twenty-four hours," I said as I pulled away from the kiss.

"Oh yeah?" he smiled. I knew he wouldn't be smiling after I told him that I didn't want to be with him.

"I think we should just be friends," I said, and I held my breath.

"Okay, cool," he said and walked away.

He made things so hard for me. He just said okay. I knew he wanted to say more, but it is what it is. I forgot I rode with him. I had to ride all the way back with him. This shit was crazy. I went back to join everyone. Dozer wasn't at the table, and I was kind of happy he wasn't. Joyce was in the kitchen, and Riah and Fizz were on the couch. Nikki was just walking in from outside.

"Fizz, Dozer wants you," she said. Apparently, he was outside. I knew I should have waited until we got back to end it. I looked at Nikki, and she smiled.

"Looks like I will be driving Fizz's car back with you guys," she said.

"What? Why?" Riah asked.

"We will talk more in the car. I don't want my mom hearing what I have to say."

We hugged Joyce goodbye, and she asked if I could make it next Sunday for dinner. I told her I had to check my schedule. I didn't want to say I wasn't coming.

We got in Fizz's car to head to our homes. I guess Dozer couldn't stand to be in the car with me. As soon as we got in the car, Riah asked why she couldn't ride with Fizz. I was laughing. She loved that man so much.

"You will see him at home. All you doing is riding with me, sis," Nikki laughed.

"So what happened? What's wrong with Dozer?" Riah asked from the back seat.

"His heart is just broken. He'll be okay," Nikki said.

"His heart is broken? Why? What you do, Deedee?" Riah asked.

"I ended it. Things aren't what they should be, and I just need to continue to focus on myself. I haven't even slept with him yet. I can't continue to have him waiting, especially after today with Kenda. Who knows what they've been doing…"

"Kenda… is she the one you told me about coming to his office at the club?" Riah asked.

"Yes, I do love him, but I don't know. When you got kidnapped, I wanted to be there, and he just left me out. I was supposed to be there for you, and I wasn't. I let you down again, and he got in the way of that," I said, with tears dropping from my eyes.

"Deedee, you did all that you could. Don't be so hard on yourself. I am fine, I'm not thinking about what happened. I just want to enjoy life with the people who mean the most to me."

"I know, but it's just that I wanted to be there."

We chatted a little more, and Nikki said she understood where I was coming from. She told me to be ready for thirsty bitches throwing themselves at him, and him being with someone else. It was going to be a hard pill to swallow, but I had to do it.

Nikki dropped me off at home, and I pulled my gun out, just in case. My alarm was on, but you never know. I ran a hot bath and got my clothes out for tomorrow. I had a lot to do tomorrow. I knew my desk was stacked with paperwork that I needed to complete. It was cool, though. I needed to keep busy. I took the longest bath and played my favorite song by Maxwell.

*L*ast night, Fizz and I made love all over the house. He actually listened to his mother and used a condom. I'm happy I was on birth-control. I went and got the shot after the first time he didn't use a condom.

After I had put him to sleep, I grabbed my phone and went downstairs to the kitchen. I grabbed an apple and laid down on the couch. I just wanted to enjoy some peace and quiet. My phone vibrated, and it was Mina. She asked if I could talk in private. Since Fizz was sleep I texted her yeah.

"Hey Ray, how are you doing?" she asked.

"I'm good. How are you? Have you been thinking about what happened?" I asked her.

"Yes… here and there, but it had to happen. My mom talked with me briefly about it. She said my dad doesn't know who did it, but Chris's uncle put out a missing report on him. His uncle told the police that Chris was into all type of shit… stuff I knew nothing about, so they think it was something to do with drugs. My mom said that she wouldn't tell my dad, though, but she wants me to stay low for a while. She said y'all should do the same, even though she said nothing is leading back to Fizz and them.

"Okay, I'll tell Fizz. Thanks, Mina. I can't believe that shit happened. That shit felt like a movie."

"I know, and I try not to think about it. Like really… my boyfriend kidnapped my best friend, but you know what? There was so much about Chris that I should've just left him, especially after putting his hands on me. I told my mom that, and she said if he wasn't already dead, she would've killed him herself. Enough about that, though. Let's just not talk about him anymore. I wanted to tell you Mo called. He wants you to meet him for lunch so y'all can talk. He heard it's a price over his head. Did you know that?" she asked.

"No, I didn't. I mean, I know Fizz was still looking for him, but they move in silence. I usually don't hear about shit until after it's over and done with."

"Well, can you meet him? I honestly think he didn't know Chris was going to do all that. Yes, he's wrong for leaving, but just hear him out. I can go with you."

"I'll go, because he keeps texting me, and you're damn right you are going with me."

******

That next day, I was on my way to meet Mo and Mina out for lunch. I jumped in my Honda, even though Fizz told me to drive his car. I didn't want him knowing what I was doing. Fizz had a full day of business he had to attend to, so I knew I wouldn't see him until late that night.

Once I made it to Applebee's, Mina was already there. I walked in and found her. We chatted for a minute, and Mo walked in. He had on a fitted cap and some glasses. He was actually looking kind of sexy.

"So, am I going to make it out of here alive?" he asked and hugged me.

"No, you're not, if you don't start talking," I said.

"Chris called me up, saying 'man, I need you to help me pull this prank on Riah'. He was actually laughing. I asked him what prank. That's when he said to pretend like we were kidnapping you. When you started swinging, I was going to say forget it, because you hit me in my damn eye. I swear I didn't know he was legit trying to pull off a real kidnapping. When he told me, I told him to let you go. He pulled his gun on me when I was going to untie you myself. I know I was wrong for just leaving you, but I wasn't thinking. I didn't want to be involved in that shit. I didn't make it right, and I am so sorry, Riah. I swear I am. I hear his uncle put out a missing report on him. Did Fizz kill him?" he asked.

"No," I said, short and sweet.

"So him disappearing had nothing to do with him or his brother?"

"No."

"Why is there a price over my head? I heard this shit from the streets myself."

"I don't know. I didn't know that until Mina told me last night. Look, I believe you, but you did leave me. Although I am fine, what if he did something to me or whoever?"

"I know, and I've been thinking about that these last few days. I wouldn't have been able to live with myself if something happened to you."

"Mo, I don't know what to do, but to tell you to stay low. I'll try to stay on Fizz and let you know what we're doing regarding you. I hate that it happened this way."

"I know… and again, I'm so sorry. I'm moving into my dorms Wednesday. I start football practice, so I have to get ready for that. I wished I didn't have to worry about this shit, though."

I started to feel bad. I didn't know what I could do. I didn't want to tell Fizz that I met with Mo because he would really want to kill him.

"I'm happy we got this out the way. I just want us to move forward. I'm moving into my own apartment, also. My mom didn't want me moving in a dorm, but whatever. That's me, but I'll only be like thirty minutes from you, Ray. I still can't believe you don't want to stay with him," she said. I gave her that look like 'you're talking too much.'

"Stay with who?" Mo asked.

"Nobody. Well, good luck on your journey. I may come to some of your games," I said, looking at him.

"Thanks. That means a lot to me."

Mina and I finished eating once Mo left. We talked about Fizz, and she started asking about Killa. I told her that he was feeling her, and she started blushing. I laughed, and we decided to have a girls' night at Deedee's this weekend.

I decided to take care of some business. I called my mom on the way to the restaurant, and I was going to chill with them later at her house. I had Mo on my mind, and I didn't want to think about that. I had to figure out a way to ask Fizz what the status was on him.

I signed up for the apartment I wanted, and the girl behind me was actually cool, so we decided to just be roommates. Her program was different than mine, and she had a lot on her plate. She was also pursuing being a photographer on the side, so she said she may only be there a few times. She worked full-time and had a shit load of classes. I didn't mind one bit, because that meant I would have more privacy. She gave me her number and wanted to hang sometime. I told her that I would, and that I'd love for her to meet my other friend.

I made it to my mom's, and Rico ran right up to me as soon as I got in the house. We played a few games, and my mom asked if I could meet her man on Friday. I wanted to say no, but I needed to be supportive of her. I told her that I would meet him. She was on a straight path, and I wanted to keep her there.

I talked with my mom after Rico went to sleep about what happened with Chris. I just needed everyone on the same page. I didn't need the police to come knocking down doors later on. I told her about Mo, and she told me not to get myself involved with that. She didn't believe that Mo could be so innocent in all of that.

She asked me about sex, and I was honest with her. I didn't like lying. I decided it was time for me to go. It was becoming late, and Fizz already told me not to be driving so late at night. I only talked to him once today. I didn't even know if he was at home or not. I kissed my mom goodbye, and she walked me to my car.

"I'm so proud of you, Riah."

"Thanks, mom… for everything."

"Call me as soon as you get home."

"Okay, I will. Love you."

I drove home in silence. Mo came across my mind a few times. I called him just to chat. I couldn't imagine how he was feeling. We started talking about Mina's ass and how funny she was. She tried so hard to hook him and me up. He told me that Amber was pregnant by some dude, and she didn't plan to go to college. I laughed so hard. We agreed to hook up for lunch soon. I pulled up and punched the code into our gate. I really loved this house. It was too damn big. I parked in the garage and walked into the house. I had just hung up with Mo right before I got out the car.

Fizz was in the kitchen, eating cereal. I laughed, because he was so crazy.

"Why are you eating cereal this late? I could've made you something if you were hungry."

"I just like eating cereal, no matter what type of food I got in the fridge," he said.

"Okay, that's different, but to each his own."

"Who were you talking to on the phone," he asked. Damn, did he have cameras watching me? I didn't know if I should try to lie or not. I was nervous. He looked at me with those damn green eyes, looking so sexy. I opened my mouth to talk when his phone rang. Saved by the fucking bell, I thought to myself.

"What's up, bro?"

"Damn, on my way now."

"Where you going this late?" I asked.

"I have to go take care of something, I'll be back in a few hours," he said as he walked away and kissed my forehead.

"A few hours? I haven't seen you all day, and you're about to leave now?" I asked, trying not to get pissed.

"Look, Ray… it's going to be a lot of late nights for a while, but just know I'm making moves to pay for this big ass house we're living in. Well… that I'll be living in."

"Don't try to play me. You know why I said I wanted to be on my own. We could've gotten a smaller house that was cheaper. Why we need this big ass mansion anyway?" I asked. I'd rather we had something we could afford that didn't require for him to be out so late. It was past midnight, and he was about to leave the house.

"Please don't argue with me, baby. I have to go. Can I get a kiss?" he asked. I kissed him, and he left. I locked up and put the alarm on. I showered and watched TV. I was happy the cable got hooked up this morning. Otherwise, I would've been bored. I called Deedee to see what she was doing. She told me she couldn't sleep. I asked what was wrong. She said nothing really. I knew it had to be about Dozer. I wished they'd both quit playing and just be together. I hung up with her and only an hour went by. I called Fizz, and his phone went to voicemail. I called again, and he answered.

"Really, Ray? Why you ain't sleep?" he asked me.

"Because my man ain't next to me in the bed."

"So what you gon' do when you living on your own."

I thought about that, and he was right. I loved being around him, but I had to do what I had to.

"You know what? Bye! I was just checking on your smart ass."

I hung up and just laid there. He had some nerve, throwing that shit back in my face. I decided to call Nikki. I hoped she wasn't sleeping.

"Hey, baby. What's up?" she asked.

"Nothing… you sleep?"

"Sleep? Girl, I just got in from the salon. I'm about to shower, eat, and go to sleep."

"Dang, look at you. Well, your brother is out, of course. He said this is how it's going to be for a while."

"Well he isn't lying, but it comes with the lifestyle."

"I know, but I'd rather he be here with me, playing with my 'you know what,'" I said as I laughed.

"Girl, you done got some dick and been showing out," she commented with a laugh.

"Just call me tomorrow. I need to go look for a job, because I be bored. Even when classes start, I'll have some free time."

"Well, this girl's hair I was doing just opened up her own clothing store. She needs some help. I can tell her you're interested, if you are?"

"Yes, that would be great."

"Okay, I'll hit her up tomorrow. She's probably going to want to meet with you, so make sure you're free."

"Thank you so much. Get some rest," I said, happy that I called her. I laid down and dozed off, pissed that Fizz still wasn't back, nor did he call back.

$\mathcal{W}$e had eight shipments come in, and we needed to distribute that shit fast. I had my crew working overtime. The numbers we were pulling in last month damn near tripled this month. I could walk away and be straight for life, but I needed it all. I had to make sure my whole family was straight, even my team.

When Riah called me, I knew she was going to be tripping. She needed to learn this was my lifestyle, and that caused late nights. We ended up at one of our stash houses. It was after four in the morning, and I knew Riah was going to be even madder. I promised to get her something nice, though. Once I planned her graduation, she would be even happier.

One of my people spotted Mo. He was moving like he didn't have a care in the world. I told them to keep tabs on him. I needed to see if the thought in the back of my mind was true, so keeping him alive for a minute was the plan. I had to admit, I was missing my baby. She wanted to be so independent. I still had to get her a car. I knew exactly what I was going to get her, too. After we finished, I talked with Killa and Dozer for a minute. Dozer wanted to grab a bite to eat. I was down.

We ended up at the waffle house. Killa asked about Mina, and I told him what was up with her. He wanted her bad. He wanted to get her alone. I told him the graduation ceremony I was planning for Riah would be perfect because she would be there.

"Man, look over there. That's the Michelle girl I was telling you about," Dozer said. I looked back, and she was bad. Her ass was fat as hell. He told me Kiya broke up with him, so I knew he was gone make his move on ol' girl.

"Damn, bro. You better jump on that. Damn... and her girls look fine as fuck, too," I mentioned.

"Hell yeah. Get them hoes over here," Killa said. Dozer walked over to Michelle, and her eyes lit up once she noticed him. She got up and hugged him. Dozer was telling the girls she was with something. They turned around and smiled. They got up and walked over with him.

"This is my brother, Fizz, and this my homie, Killa," Dozer said, introducing us.

"Killa... that sounds scary," Michelle laughed.

"Well, I think it's sexy... just like him," one of her friends said, eyeing him like she wanted to fuck.

"This is Michelle's friend, Jordan, and this is Charm," he said. Charm was real pretty. She was neck and neck with Riah, but Riah had way more ass than her. Jordan was cute, too. She was more interested in Killa. They sat down, and we all just chatted. Michelle and Dozer were having their own conversation, and so were Jordan and Killa. Charm was making small talk, but I didn't want to take it there with her, knowing I had a girl. She was sexy with those full lips. She just openly stared at me.

"What's up, sweetheart? You just gon' keep staring at a nigga?" I asked.

"Sorry, I just love your face," she replied. I raised my eyebrows, not sure of what to say to that. I mean, who wouldn't love this face.

"I'm sorry. What I meant is that I'm pursuing photography. I try to capture everything. Some things are just so beautiful, you have to take a picture to keep the memory of it," she explained.

"Oh yeah? That's deep," I smiled at her, liking her style.

"Yes. If I had my camera out, I would be taking so many pictures of you. Your smile and those dimples are just simply beautiful," she said as she stared away at me. I licked my lips out of habit and nodded my head up and down. Damn, she was sexy. I needed to dismiss myself, because she was turning me on.

She asked what I did for a living, and I told her about my businesses. She asked if she could take pictures of the cars I painted. I told her she could. Then, she asked for my number. We exchange numbers. She talked more about cars. I must admit, I never met a girl who was interested in cars like her. I wondered if she had a man. It didn't matter, because I had a girl. I told Dozer I had to get going, so I dropped him and Killa off at home. I needed to run home, shower, and head to the recreation center for this project we had going on.

It was close to seven-thirty in the morning when I got home. Riah was still sleep when I walked into the room. I was happy, because I didn't feel like arguing with her little ass. I walked into my closet and grabbed a button-down shirt and some slacks. I quickly dressed. I grabbed my socks and put on my shoes. I came out the closet, shut the door, and Riah was standing right there.

"Good morning, beautiful," I said as I kissed her cheeks.

"What time you make it in?"

"Here we go," I said, walking away.

"Mothafucka, that ain't no answer," she stated.

"Who the fuck you talking to like that? You better watch your mouth. I just got in, and I have to go back out to the center."

She turned around and went into the bathroom. There wasn't much I could say. There were going to be days like this. Yes, I could've come home after business, but shit, I didn't. I heard the shower running, so she was in the shower. I went downstairs and grabbed my papers from my office. Maria did a great job of organizing everything for me.

"So you just got in, showered, and now you about to leave again? There ain't that much business to keep you that damn busy," she commented. I don't know how her ass kept creeping up unannounced.

"Yes, Riah... all of that," I said.

"Wow."

She walked away, and I grabbed her.

"Baby, don't be mad at daddy. I'll make it up to you. I promise," I said as I tongued her down. She didn't hesitate to kiss me back. I loved kissing her. The kiss was getting tense, and I knew I had to leave.

"Let me get some dick before you go," she smiled.

"I hate to turn you down, but I really have to go, sexy. I will see you later tonight, okay?"

"Later tonight... again?" she asked.

"Baby, please don't make me feel any worse than I already do. You think I like being away from you?"

"Whatever, Fizz. See you later."

I kissed her forehead and left. I needed to be on time to meet with these people on this project. It could bring major paper to the center if the deal went through. I stopped and thought about Riah for a minute. I hadn't even asked what she had planned for today. I would call her around lunch time and check on her. I called Nikki and asked if she and Mina could help with planning a ceremony for Riah. She agreed she would.

Dozer

I was in my office at the car wash. I had to be over at the club in about forty-five minutes to get the final touches set-up for Naz's welcome home party for next weekend. Everything was coming together; I had my promoters on the job. I invited Michelle out that night. She said she was excited. I couldn't wait, either. We hadn't had sex yet, even though she'd been throwing it at me. I told her we should get to know each other, first. I guess when she found out I didn't want to just hit it, she calmed down a little bit, but I could tell she wanted me bad. Shit, I wanted to fuck her ass, too. Something was just holding me back, and I knew what it was. She invaded my thoughts all day, but I had to remember she didn't want me.

My phone rang, and I answered. It was Riah.

"Sup, sis?"

"Your dumb ass brother. Where were y'all at last night?" she said in the phone.

"Riah, talk to him. Why you calling me about his whereabouts?" I said softly.

"I don't know why I called you. You're gon' side with him, regardless," she said, and hung up. I laughed to myself, because calling me was pointless. My lil' sis was crazy. I told my receptionist I was out for the rest of the day. She knew how to operate, so I was good.

I made it to the club, and my phone vibrated again. I answered as

I got out the car. It was my sweet chocolate calling.

"Hey, sexy," I said.

"Hey, baby. What you up to?

"At the club, about to finalize the plans for my homie's welcome home party. You know… the party I invited you to?"

"Oh yeah. Well, can I see you tonight? Maybe you can come to my spot. We can watch something on Netflix and chill."

"Okay, that sounds cool. It'll be later, though, like eight-thirty."

"Okay, that's cool. I really don't cook, so I'll order Chinese if that's cool."

"Yeah, that's straight. I'll see you then."

I hung up and thought damn, she don't cook… the fuck?

I talked with the people about the party. I got some mail, so I went up to my office to open it. It wasn't anything important. It was just some licenses I needed to renew. I passed that along to the manager to handle. I had a slight headache, because I wasn't really sleeping through the night. I closed my eyes for a minute, and there was a knock at my door. I shook my head with my eyes still closed. I couldn't get a piece of mind for shit.

"Come in."

My eyes were still closed. When I heard my door being locked, I opened them quickly and grabbed my gun.

"It's just me, daddy."

"You can't be serious right now."

"Look, I'm sorry for everything. I can't help that you drive me crazy."

"Crazy isn't the word for you."

"Let me just please you, and I'll leave. I promise."

I just stared at her. She came up there with a dress on, and I could tell she didn't have any panties on. I watched her come closer and unbuckle my pants. She pulled out my dick and went to work. I thought about the shit for a minute and pushed her away.

"Look, Kenda... I can't take it there with you anymore. Please leave, and stop coming up to my office. You're welcome to party, but that's it. Now leave.

"That ugly bitch got your nose wide open," she said, referring to Kiya.

"Bye, Kenda! This was your last and final warning."

She left out, and I followed her back down to the floor. She got in her car and pulled off. Damn, I was that close, but I couldn't betray Nikki like that again.

Fizz called and said he wanted to plan Riah's ceremony for Saturday. I told him whatever he needed, I was there. I knew Kiya would be there. I thought about bringing Michelle, but knew better than to right now. She might as well get use to seeing us together, though.

I called my mom and told her the bad news, because Michelle would soon be doing Sunday dinners.

"Hey, Mom."

"Hey, baby. How are you?"

"I'm doing okay. I called to tell you something before you find out by someone else."

"Don't tell me Kiya's pregnant. Oh my God! I'm going to be a grandmother, finally."

"What? No, she isn't pregnant. You gave Fizz a hard time about that, so now you want a grandbaby?"

"Well, Riah is still wet behind her ears, but De'Kiya has established a lot. She is most definitely ready."

I hated to say what I needed to, but I had to.

"Mom, Kiya and I broke up," I said and waited for her response. When she didn't say anything, I decided to say something.

"I did meet someone else. I think you'll really like her just as much as Kiya."

"I know damn well you ain't run off and find some other trick. Boy, you should be trying to get your girl back. I swear you and Fizz… for y'all to be so smart, y'all act so damn crazy. Get your ass off my phone," she said, and hung up. I laughed so hard, because my mom was so funny. She was probably praying to God right now for forgiveness for cursing me out. If only she knew I tried making it work with Kiya. She left me. I called Fizz to tell him about his mama.

Deedee

I was in my office when my boss, Steven, knocked on my door. He brought me more paperwork, of course. Then, he came right back in. I wanted to say 'look, do I look like a damn robot'? I was so off my A-game today. It was ridiculous.

"De'Kiya, I would like for you to meet Desmond. He is our newest marketing member, and he also has some background in finance. I asked that he work with you so that when you are off or on vacation, he can help fill in," he said.

I was happy to hear that. I needed a damn vacation, starting now.

"Okay, where is he?" I asked. He picked up my phone and asked the secretary to send him in my office. Once he made it in, my head was down.

"De'Kiya, this is Desmond. He likes to be called Dez. Desmond, this is De'Kiya, the hardest worker here," Steven said as he introduced us. This man was fine, but his swag was a little off. I got up and shook his hand. His cologne invaded my noise, and it smelled so good.

"Likewise," he said, as he shook my hand.

"I'll let you two talk and get acquainted. Maybe you can decide on a schedule to train him on a few things this week," Steven mentioned.

"Sure," I said. Steven walked out and Desmond turned back to me. I instructed him to have a seat. Once he did, I asked where he was from. He was from here. I wondered if he knew of Dozer.

"So you really like it here?" I heard him say, breaking me from my thoughts.

"Yes, I really do. I think you will, too."

"Well, I do now. At first, I didn't see any African Americans here until he introduced us. I started to feel better about the decision I made to accept the offer," he smiled.

"Yes, it's nice to see someone else of color, I must admit."

We just kind of stared at each other for a minute. I broke the silence and showed him what I was doing. He showed me a few tricks also, which cut my time in half to get the finance reports finished. He asked to take half of my load, and at first, I declined, but he insisted it wasn't a problem. We worked through lunch, so we ordered in. We had most of the financial reports done. Now, we had to create the analysis on all of the accounts.

"You know if you do a periodic check on these accounts and this number here matches this number, you can divide this by this, and add these two rolls up to get the total," he said as he bent over me, pointing at my computer. He was so smart, and I was happy someone was helping me. We looked up, and it was almost seven at night.

"Wow, it's late, and I am starving," I said.

"Would you like to grab a bite to eat?" he asked.

He hadn't hit on me, so I knew it was strictly business. I accepted his offer. We decided on Chinese. We headed downtown. I was following behind him when Riah called my phone. She was complaining about Fizz's late nights, and I assured her it was because of business only. She said her apartment was ready and furnished. She went out and got a new bed, because she didn't want to sleep on the one there. I didn't blame her. She asked where I was, and I told her, in a way. I just said some co-workers and I were grabbing food. I hung up with her just in time for me to get out and walk in the restaurant with Desmond.

We waited to be seated. We laughed and joked about some of the people coming in and out. When our table was ready, we ordered. He told me where he worked before, and I'm happy he left his previous employer, because they were in the middle of bankruptcy. When I told him, he was shocked. We'd been seated for a while and still hadn't seen a waiter.

"Hey, I'm going to go ask what's taking so long. Be right back," he said, as he got up. I couldn't hear him after he got past the fourth table, but I could slightly see him. I looked at my phone and played a few games until he got back. It seemed like it was taking him forever just to talk with someone. This was my last time coming here. I heard they were under new management, but damn. What was he doing... trying to get the place shut down? We had been there an hour and still hadn't ordered. I was becoming impatient.

#

$\mathcal{I}$ was picking up the Chinese that Michelle had ordered. They were busy as fuck. I stood in the line to pick up my food when a guy came to the counter, demanding to talk with the manager. When the manager finally did come out, I could tell the brother was trying to be professional as possible.

"Hello, sir. I hear you requested to talk to me?" the manager said.

"Yes, the lady and I over there been here an hour, and no one has taken our orders yet, I just want to know what type of service this is. I mean, I know it's busy, but—"

"Yes, we are very busy, but I will personally take your order. We had staff quit today," the manager said. I peeked around to see who his girl was. I couldn't believe my fucking eyes. I tried to stay calm, because maybe, just maybe it was a business dinner. She was dressed in work attire, and so was the guy.

The manager walked back, and another lady came to the front, giving out the pickup orders. She finally got to me and that's when the manager came back out. The guy walked back to the table and I watched the manager talk and write down their orders. I already had our food, but I couldn't stop watching her. She was smiling at whatever he was saying. I got pissed and walked away.

In the car, I couldn't help but feel like she played me. I didn't know that exactly, but that's how I felt. I decided to call her to see if she would answer. She did, in fact, send me to voicemail. It was all good though. I got to Michelle's crib. We ate and watched movies as planned. She started rubbing her hands on my dick. I wasn't going to deny her the dick tonight. She pulled it out and started sucking on it. Man, that shit felt so good. I started to pump in and out of her mouth. She deep throated my dick, and I tried to push her away before I busted, but she swallowed every last drop. She pulled out a condom and tried to put it on me. I wasn't going for that though. I had my own condom I didn't need a few months from now her telling me she was pregnant.

I had her lay on her back with her leg spread apart. She did what I told her. Once I put the condom on, I slid inside of her. Her shit was so wet. She put her legs on top of my shoulders and I started pumping faster and harder, making her moan.

"Oh yes, daddy...just like that...oh yes, I'm about to cum."

"Yeah, cum for daddy, baby," I said, and that made her cum hard as hell. She was moaning so loud. She pulled me down to kiss her. I pecked her lips while she tried to tongue me down. Kiya was the first girl I had kissed in a while. I really like Michelle, but I didn't want to kiss her just yet. I know she noticed that I didn't kiss her back. She wanted to ride me, so I let her. She rode my dick like a champ, making my toes curl up.

After both of us coming three times, I washed up and tried to leave.

"So you going to leave me lonely tonight?" she asked.

"Yeah, I have a busy day tomorrow. I have to be up early."

"I wanted to make you breakfast in the morning and wake you up with some fye head."

I didn't want to turn her down, but I did need to get home. I promised her I would spend the night on the weekend. I left and headed home. Once I got in. I checked my phone to see if Kiya called back. She hadn't. I just needed to leave her alone. It was obvious that she really moved on, so I said fuck her and planned to do the same.

Nikki

$\mathcal{F}$izz had asked that I help him with putting a ceremony together for Riah. Of course I said yeah. She was going to be so happy. That was the sweetest thing my brother could've had done. Mina, Kiya, and I were at the store, getting things for the ceremony. I already had the stage for the set-up. It was going to be at their house in their big ass back yard. The party was tomorrow, and we still had more to do. Fizz said she'd been staying at her apartment, so he hadn't seen much of her. They were so crazy. They couldn't leave each other's side, but stayed in separate houses.

We grabbed a bite to eat. Riah had called all three of us, but we couldn't let her know what we were doing, or that we were with each other. We left and went to the mall. Of course we shopped until we dropped, especially Mina. That girl was worse than me. Even Kiya switched her style up. I waited until we dropped Mina off and asked about her and my brother. She said they still weren't together. He had mentioned he was talking to someone else. I didn't want to betray him and tell her that. We chatted up until I dropped her off. She said she was going to take a long nap. I didn't blame her. We'd been out since this morning, and it was close to dinner time.

I was in my basement, working out, and listening to music when Dozer walked in. I laughed at him. I could see it in his eyes. Either he wanted me to do his hair, or he was going to ask about Kiya.

"Sup?" I asked, taking the ear buds out my ear.

"She got another man. I got info on that nigga I saw her with. He works with her. He graduated top of his class, so that's what she likes?"

"What are you talking about?" I asked him.

"Sis, I know you know. I know you and her got this friendship thing, but don't forget who your loyalty lies with."

"Dozer, get out of your fucking feelings, first of all. You're acting real tender right now. Second, I didn't know anything about another guy. She ain't said shit to me about another nigga. We were just together, and I asked her about you. She said y'all were still broken up. That's all she said."

"Well, stop asking her, because we are completely done. I want you to meet someone though. Her name is Michelle," he said.

"Nah, bro. I'm straight," I confessed. I knew my brother. Whoever this chick is, she was just something to pass time by, because deep down, he was hoping Kiya come back.

"Man, you worse than your mama," he laughed. We chatted a bit more, and he said he invited her to come to Nazir's welcome home party next weekend. My heart started racing. Time was moving fast. He was almost home. Dozer was still talking, and I hadn't heard a word he said. The last thing I heard was Nazir.

Once Dozer left, I bathed and chilled on my couch, watching TV, since I had to clear my schedule to help with the ceremony for tomorrow. I decided to just chill. I started thinking about Mason's letter that he left me. That's why I needed to keep busy. I hadn't told anyone, because some stuff you just take to your grave. It wasn't even ten at night yet, and I was getting sleepy. My phone vibrated, and it was him. I was just thinking about him, and he was calling. I waited for him to get on the phone, and then said hello.

"Nikki, I don't have long now, baby," he said as if he was smiling. I knew he had to be happy about it. I was happy for him. He walked that time down like a G.

"I'm happy for you. I know you are ready to come home."

"Yeah, I can't wait to come home," he said. I honestly think he was saying home as in my home, but I dismissed that thought.

"Did Fizz tell you about his girl?" I asked, changing the subject.

"Man, did he? I saw pictures of her and everything. She bad, but she ain't on your level, though. I haven't met a female that was, to be honest."

Damn he had to just throw that in there. I didn't know what to say to him, so I said what came to mind.

"Aww, that's sweet."

He chuckled a little. It was kind of quiet. I hated this awkward silence.

"So my mom asked about you. She said that she can't wait to put some meat on your bones, because she knows you're probably skinny now," I laughed.

"Man, I miss my mama. How she been doing?" he asked.

"She's doing great."

"That's good. I have to make sure I go see her."

"You better, or you know you won't hear the end of it," I told him.

"I already know. I can't wait to see you, either."

"Yes umm, me either. I know you have some crazy stories to tell," I managed to say.

"Oh, you already know, but I'll see you soon, Nikki. Be good, baby."

We hung up, and I was happy. Nazir would always have my heart, but sometimes, you just had to move on. I just hoped I could be true to my word once he was out.

I have been staying in my apartment for a few days now. With the money Fizz gave me, I bought a whole new wardrobe. I got the job at the clothing store. Nikki had talked with the girl, Ann, about letting me work there. My classes started in another week, so I could train and work whenever she needed me to.

I hadn't seen much of Fizz lately, and it is what it is. He basically called when he wanted to. He got mad and asked why I hadn't been calling him. Shit, when somebody keeps saying they're busy every time you call, it's best just to wait until they have time for you. He said he had a surprise for me. I knew it was going to be a new car. What else could it be?

My roommate came in. We did lunch one day, and she was really cool. I could see myself hanging with her. She was so funny. She took like a million pictures of me, saying I was beautiful and all of that. She told me about some guy she met. She did mention he had a brother, but I remembered her saying he talks to her friend. I told her I had a man, but she didn't believe me because I was always there. She had a point, though. I invited her out for Fizz's home boy's welcome home party next weekend. She was excited to come. I told her to leave that damn camera at home.

I was about to call my mom when Fizz called.

"Hello?"

"Where you at?" he asked.

"At home," I answered back.

"Your home is here. Speaking of home, you haven't been here. What's up with you? You've been tripping lately," he said. This nigga had some nerve, like he was even around to know I was tripping. I just sat on the phone.

"Come home so you can ride my dick. I miss your little sexy self," he said, making me blush.

"I'll be there."

I hung up and decided to go see him. After all, that's why I'd been tripping, for his attention.

Once I made it home, I parked my car and went inside. He was texting and cheesing with somebody. I knew it wasn't a nigga having him cheese like that. That was that 'girl you crazy' smile.

"So who you texting?" I asked, walking up to him.

"A friend, but come here," he said, as he tongued me down. That kiss was just what I needed. He was looking so sexy, too. We went up to our bedroom, and our clothes were already off before we made it up.

"You miss daddy?" he asked.

"Of course," I said, waiting for him to eat me out. He started kissing my pussy, giving me exactly what I wanted. I was so addicted to this man that it was crazy.

"Oh yes…I like that, baby," I said. He inserted his tongue inside of me. He rolled his tongued all up in my pussy. This nigga had my head gone. Once he made me come, I was ready to ride him… something else I had learned. I didn't know how good at it I was going to be, but I hope he liked it. I started moving slowly, making myself comfortable at first. I started moving up and down, giving him more pleasure. I started moving my hips, watching him close his eyes, letting me know he was enjoying it.

"Damn, Ray…you doing your thing, baby."

I started lifting up and down with more speed, watching his dick disappear inside of me.

"Ahh… don't make me cum yet…Ahh, yes! Damn! My bad, Ray. I couldn't hold it any longer."

"No need to apologize, baby. That's exactly what I wanted."

We laid there in each other's arms for a good forty-five minutes. I got up to shower, and he came in the shower with me. He kissed me, and I hugged him. I wanted it to be just like that all the time… just him and me.

Once out the shower, we dressed and left. I was so happy at that moment. He took me out to eat and shopping again. I only bought shoes that time, though. I had Nikki press my hair the other day and wrap it. I was working a middle part. My shit looked fake, but it was real.

"So Riah, what's been up? Talk to me. You a working woman now, doing your thing? I don't get to see you that much now that you are working."

"You didn't see me when I wasn't doing shit, so there's not much difference," I confessed.

"You know you don't have to work. I got you."

"I don't want to always have to depend on you, Fizz, and besides… I like my job."

He looked over at me. I kept his ass speechless. He took me to get my nails and feet done. He was really spoiling me today. I knew it was because he felt bad that we weren't spending time together.

I started thinking about my whole attitude about being independent, when the only thing I had was an apartment that my scholarship basically paid for. I did get a job, though. I felt like I was depending too much on Fizz. I didn't want to be like those other girls. Maybe I was over thinking it. He was my man, and I knew that he didn't mind doing the things he did for me. I loved him for who he was, not what he had. I asked him to get his feet done with me. He made me laugh so hard. He was so ticklish. The lady told him he couldn't come back. He was that bad. He jumped completely out the seat while she tried scrubbing his feet. He had some pretty feet, if I do say so myself. I wondered what else he had in store for me. I wished he would show me the car already, because I knew that's what my surprise was.

We got in the car, and he asked about Mo. I didn't want to have that conversation, because it was going to just cause an argument between us.

"You ain't heard shit from that nigga, Mo?"

"Why you asking me that?"

"Because I want to know. Ain't that why you ask questions?"

"Well, don't you think I would tell you if I did?" I asked.

"Why you always get so defensive when I bring that nigga's name up?"

"Really? I am not about to go there with you," I said as I rolled my eyes.

"So you gon' front like that? I noticed how tense you get every time his name comes up. What… you don't want your little boyfriend to die?" he teased.

"You sound stupid. I just think he didn't have a major part in it, as I said before. Yes, he helped kidnap me, but he thought it was a prank. Mo isn't anything like Chris," I disclosed.

"So what you saying is, you don't want him to die?"

"I mean—"

"He's going to die, Riah, and that's a promise," he revealed.

I just shook my head and looked out the window. Talking to him about it wasn't going to save Mo's life. I didn't know what to do. How was I supposed to stop Fizz from killing him? I thought about talking to Nikki. She understood me better than he did.

We pulled up to the house and waited for the gate to open. I noticed a few cars lined up in our roundabout driveway. I wondered what everyone was doing here.

"Why is everyone here?" I asked.

"I forgot to tell you, we're having a little barbecue for a house warming," he confessed.

"I wished you would have told me. I really don't feel like being around anyone," I mentioned as I got out of the car.

"So you're feeling some type of way because I'm going to kill your little boyfriend," he taunted. I looked at him and got out of the car. Who jokes about killing someone? Chris and Mason deserved that shit, but Mo really didn't. I walked into the house, and Fizz grabbed me.

"Look… my fault. I shouldn't be saying that shit to you. Come here," he said as he hugged me. I looked into his eyes. I wanted to be honest with him, but I didn't' want him thinking that I wanted Mo, because I didn't. We walked into the house and I heard music. It seemed like it was coming from outside. I guess some family time would be nice, but why would he take me out to eat if we were having a barbecue?

I went upstairs to freshen up, Fizz picked out a dress for me. I thought it was too much for a BBQ, but I put it on anyway. I put on my necklace and charm bracelet. Fizz watched as I finished dressing. I walked up to him and kissed him. He just didn't know how I wanted to fuck him right now. He said I'd been doing my thing in the bed, but I wanted to make all his fantasies come true. We kissed for what seemed like forever, when we heard someone clear their throat behind us.

"Do y'all always have to kiss… like we trying to eat, and y'all having a make out session?" Dozer laughed.

"Were coming down now, bro," Fizz said. I walked past Dozer to head down the stairs.

"Damn, sis, can I get a hug, kiss, or something?" Dozer asked.

"Nope," I said, going down the steps. I was mad he wouldn't tell me what I wanted to hear last time I called him. We got downstairs, and Fizz told me to close my eyes. He directed me to the back. He said my surprise was here now. I knew it was a car. I heard the music completely stop. Fizz had his hand over my eyes. I heard Deedee talking.

"We are here to celebrate the graduating class of 2016. Riah Walts is graduating with honors," Deedee said through the microphone. My mouth dropped. I couldn't believe what I was hearing. Fizz removed his hands and they had a little ceremony all set up for me. I was so speechless.

"Will all the graduates stand up as we are ready to call you up," Deedee said. I walked toward the stage. When Deedee called my name, I walked up and received my diploma. I started crying. This was so amazing that they did all of this for me. Everyone started clapping and hollering my name. Rico ran up to me and hugged me tightly. I hugged my mom and Deedee. Joyce was there which meant the world to me. I noticed Dozer looking at Deedee, but she wouldn't even look his way. He mentioned to Fizz about having to leave in a bit to pick up his girl for their date. I know Deedee heard it, because I heard it, and he was right next to me.

I knew I had to make a speech. I thanked everyone and especially Fizz. Just when I thought it was all over, Fizz told me to close my eyes again.

"Open your eyes, baby," Fizz said.

I opened my eyes, and it was a brand new Black and pink Bentley.

"Fizz, OMG, you did not get me a Bentley," I said, as I ran to the car. It was black with pink trimming. I wasn't a material girl, but damn. This car was most definitely a head turner.

"Wow, that is nice," Nikki said.

"Riah, can you drive that thing?" Rico asked. Everyone started laughing. Fizz told me to go for a ride. I jumped in and told Mina to get in with me. She was still speechless. We drove about ten minutes away before we turned around and came back.

"Ray, Fizz is so good to you. I'm so happy you found someone like him," she said as she started crying.

"Mina, don't cry, because then I'll cry, and I can't wait until you find someone who does the same for you."

"I doubt if I'll find someone on their level, but I just want love… true love," she confessed. We made it back to the house and walked to the back. Everyone was enjoying themselves and eating. I saw how Killa was looking at Mina.

"Mina, Killa is staring you down. I think he wants you," I said.

"Girl, is he? He is so damn sexy…I can do some things with him. Like… I can see him beating my pussy from the back," she said.

"Girl, you so nasty, but come on. Go over there with me."

We walked over, and I hugged Fizz.

"Thanks, baby. I love it. I can't wait to show you how much I appreciate everything you did today," I whispered in his ear.

"You can thank me now. I'm about to put them all out," he said as he licked my ear.

"No, we can't just put them out. I promise it'll be worth the wait," I said, as I licked his ear.

I turned around, and Killa was talking with Mina. He was all up on her. I knew he wanted her ass. We all chatted and talked. My mom and Rico left to go home. I was supposed to meet her man today, but she rescheduled, and now I know why. It was because Fizz had a whole graduation ceremony planned. Once everyone left, Fizz ran the water for the Jacuzzi on the other side of the deck. I had my robe on, and he took his clothes off, leaving nothing but his chain. I kissed him, and I knew it was going to be a wonderful night.

Mina

I had been dealing with my own issues. I often thought what if I kept the baby. Some days were better than others. After Chris did what he did, I knew I had made the right choice. I didn't want to trust anyone else. I know there are good men out there. I was so happy for Riah. She deserved everything good that happened to her. While I was at their house, Killa asked if he could call me. I told him yeah. Then, he asked if I could come home with him. It was tempting, but I wasn't for all of that. He kept pressuring me, saying he would be the perfect gentleman. I looked into his eyes. I knew he wanted the pussy, but he had to know I wasn't about to let him in my draws.

"Look I don't know about all of that, Killa, and if I do, are you going to keep your hands to yourself?" I asked.

"Yeah, I can do that," he said as he rubbed his hand down my back.

"You sure? You can't even control your hands now," I smiled.

He licked his lips, and smirked. I knew if I did, he would probably try something, but if he respected when I said no, I would be straight.

"So you gon' spend the night or what?"

"Yeah, I'll chill with you, but I don't know about spending the night," I said, as I looked at how handsome he was.

That was an hour ago. Now, we were at his house, chilling. He played the video game while music played low in the back. He had a nice house, almost as nice as Riah and Fizz. He asked if I wanted to play, and I said no. He turned it off and looked at me.

"You want a drink?" he asked.

"You got some wine? I'm not really a drinker, but I'll sip some wine if you have it," I said.

"Yeah, I got some champagne."

He got up, grabbed it, and a wine glass. He was drinking 1800 out the bottle.

"Damn, you drinking that?" I asked.

"Yeah, why you cursing? You're too pretty to have a mouth like that."

"Is it a problem that I do?"

"No, but tone it down for me if you can," he smiled.

"Yeah, I can do that, daddy!"

Shit, did I say that out loud? I didn't mean to. I just wanted to think it. Damn … I know he was probably turned on by that shit.

"Daddy? I like that. Come closer. Why you way over there?" he asked. I was sitting on the opposite end of the couch. I came closer and he looked at me. I knew he was about to kiss me from the way he was looking at me. We kissed, and he started with those damn hands again. He rubbed all over my body. It was nice to get some attention and just relax. He broke the kiss, and I was kind of mad he did.

"Let me stop before things go too far. I know you said for me to keep my hands to myself. I had to kiss you, though. Hope you didn't mind it," he said. His voice was so sexy and deep. I didn't mind the kiss at all. I actually liked it.

"No, I didn't mind. I kind of enjoyed it," I confessed.

"Straight up? So you wouldn't mind me doing it again?" he asked.

"No, I would actually like it if you do it again," I told him. He leaned over and kissed me again. I was getting hot and bothered. We kissed for a while, and he pulled away again.

"Man, I want you to ride my dick right now," he said.

"I can't, Killa. Wait… what's your real name. I can't be calling you that."

"I can't tell you that. That's classified information," he said. I laughed, but he didn't.

"Well, okay then," I said.

"I never told anyone outside my circle my name. Niggas I run with don't even remember it anyway, because I'll always be known as Killa."

"Okay, well you don't have to tell me."

I couldn't see myself fucking someone and not knowing their real name. He started kissing me again. I told him I was kind of chilly, so he gave me a throw blanket.

"You still going home, or you gon' spend the night with me?" he asked.

"I guess I can stay. My parents are out of town, so I don't want to be alone."

"You shouldn't have to be," he said.

"Tell me something about you," I said.

He leaned back, telling me basically what he wanted me to know; who he was before he met Fizz and Dozer. He got the name Killa because he killed his parents. It was never proven that he did, though. I felt so bad for him. His dad would come in his room every night and put bleach in the cup of water next to his bed. Every morning, he poured it out. His little sister wasn't so lucky, though. She died. That's when he decided to kill them to get justice for his little sister. I didn't ask him how he killed them. I really didn't want to know. He moved to Georgia with his grandpa, and he died four years later. He was only sixteen when he died, so he went to the streets, and the streets raised him. He said that's how he met Dozer, from the streets, and they've been solid ever since.

"Well, to me, it sounds like you need a woman to come home to. Why are you single, or are you?"

"Yeah, I'm single. I'm weighing my options right now. I got two bad ones on the line," he said as he winked at me. I didn't know what to say to that, but I loved competition. I wasn't ready for a serious relationship just yet, but I wanted him, and I was going to get him.

"Well, I guess I need to shut the competition down," I said, as I winked back at him.

"The ball is in your court, lil' mama," he said. We talked some more. He asked about my relationship with Chris, and I told him how bad it was. He was happy Chris couldn't hurt me anymore. He kissed me again, and this time, it went a little further than I expected.

"Damn, girl…your shit tight as hell, just like I like it," he said, pumping in and out of me. It felt so good, and I had already climaxed once. The second one was on its way. I wanted to know his name, and he was about to tell it to me.

"Tell me your name, baby, so I can yell it...oh, shit! That feels so good," I moaned. I was riding him, so I turned around and rode him reverse cow-girl style.

"Damn, girl...ahh hell...yeah, ride it just like that..."

"Tell me," I said,

"It's Tramel...Damn, ahh...I'm about to bust."

He came, and I accomplished exactly what I wanted. I didn't get to call out his name, because he was already cumming. I got off his dick and sat next to him.

"Mina, you so bad. Damn, ain't no bitch ever made me do that," he said.

"Excuse you! Please don't refer to me as a bitch," I said.

"You got it. My fault, but you better not ever give my pussy away," he expressed while pulling my hair.

"So you claiming me now?" I asked.

"Yes, I just don't tell any bitch... I mean, any girl my name."

"Tramel... that's cute. I like that better than Killa. Can I call you that?" I asked.

"Damn, look how it rolls off of your tongue. Yeah, only when it's you and me, though," he said, and kissed my lips.

I didn't expect to be his girl so soon, but whatever. It happens when you get caught by a boss. He told me a little bit more about him. He said all he wanted was my loyalty. I could give him that, plus more. He let me shower and gave me a t-shirt to put on. The shirt was drowning me. His tall ass looked like a giant compared to me.

He gave me a tour of his house. He said I could chill over any time I wanted, even when he wasn't there. His indoor swimming pool was surely going to get used by me. We made it up to his bedroom, and he told me to brush his hair for him.

"Mina, guess what?"

"What?" I asked.

"I do have a wife and kid."

I sat there, trying not to hit him in the back of the head with the brush in my hand. I got up so that I could leave.

"Where you going? I'm just messing with you," he joked.

"That wasn't funny. I don't have time for that shit," I announced.

"Aww, come here, mama. I was joking, but I was going to say that it was my plan to make you my girl. All that talk downstairs was just talk. I do have some hoes I fuck with from time to time. I will end that shit for you, though."

"You better. I don't come second to no hoe, bitch, or any other female you fucking with," I spoke.

"Watch your mouth. All that cursing isn't necessary," he said, pulling my legs, making me fall on my back. He laid in between my legs kissing my lips. He was so sexy with those big lips. I enjoyed kissing them.

"I want to get to know you more. I don't want this to just be a sexual thing," I said.

"I'm on the same shit, baby. So what school did you decide on? I heard Riah telling Fizz you haven't decided yet."

"I'm going to law school. My parents already paid my tuition. They want me to work just as hard as them. I was going to get my own apartment, but I'll be staying with my parents. They're never home anyway."

He was still on me. We just talked and chilled. I wanted to learn as much as I could about him. He had already showed me his soft side.

$\mathcal{D}$eedee

$\mathcal{I}$ was home, working on a few reports, drinking a glass of wine. I was trying not to think about Dozer. Seeing him at the graduation ceremony that Fizz put together was hard. He looked so sexy. I felt him mean mugging me. I don't know why he had this hatred all of a sudden. I hadn't spoken to him since I broke up with him. I know he meant for me to hear him say something about picking his girl up. I wasn't tripping. Shit, maybe it would be easy to get over him now that he had moved on. He moved on fast, too. A part of me wanted to know who the girl was, but my stubbornness was taking over.

I decided to put work to the side. It was the weekend, and I was in the house, bored. I wondered what Desmond was doing. He was fun to hang with, and he was attractive, but I didn't want to cross those lines, especially being that we worked together. I texted Desmond, asking about some report that I had already finished just to have an excuse to text him. He said I needed a life, and that it was the weekend. He asked me out for drink. It was about eight-thirty, so I decided I would. I got dressed and met him downtown. It was live, and people were out everywhere. We met at a bar and had a few drinks. We laughed and talked about some of the people in the office. I looked at how handsome he was and still I couldn't find the chemistry there. He wasn't someone I could be with.

We decided it was time to leave. I noticed he got excited around certain crowds that came close by us in the bar. I just put it off and continued to have a good time. I asked him to come back to my place for more talking. I told him we could play this game I had just bought. He wanted to stop at the gas station for some ice and chips first. He was really weird. As he got out, I told him to bring me something back.

I was waiting for Desmond to come out the store when Dozer's car pulled up. My heart started beating fast. I saw a female get out of car and walk in the store.

"That must be that bitch," I said out loud. Desmond came out the store, and Dozer's car door opened, letting me know he was getting out. When he stepped out, he looked my way. I swear I felt like time stopped. I pulled off. I don't know why he was looking when he had a whole bitch inside of the store. My phone vibrated. I didn't even look down to see who it was.

"Did you see that man at the gas station staring? I saw him somewhere else before. It was recently, and we were together. It had to be at the Chinese place," he stated.

"What? He was there that night?"

That could be why he ran out and got a girl.

"Did he see me?"

"I don't know. I noticed him looking that way, but who knows what he was looking at. Who is he?"

"My ex," I said, hoping he wouldn't be intimidated.

"Oh, okay. He's handsome. Why y'all break up?"

That was unusual for a guy to say, but whatever.

"I was being stubborn, basically. I just ended it."

"So he probably thinks that I'm your new man, right?" he asked.

"Yeah, he does. I know him, and that's exactly what he thinks."

"He's not crazy, is he?" he asked.

"Yeah, a little, but don't worry. I'll protect you," I laughed.

We made it back to my house, and we drank the rest of the wine I had. It was so weird with Desmond. I felt like I was chilling with one of my girls. I was open with him and just free. I told him more about my relationship with Dozer. I didn't tell him about his dark side. I basically just said he made a major decision without including me. Desmond thought I was being a bitch. I looked at my phone and saw that it was Dozer who called. Nikki showed up on my screen, and I didn't know if I wanted to answer or not. I figured I should, because she had been neutral through the whole break-up.

"Hello?"

"Can you talk?" she asked.

"Yeah, I have company, but what's up?" I asked.

"Can that person hear me?"

"Nope, you good."

"Dozer saw you and your company. He's on your ass, girl," she laughed.

"What?"

"Girl, he called Killa to come see who was at your house with you. Killa said he was in the middle of something, so Dozer threatened to kill him. Killa got to your house, saw the guy you were with, took pictures of whatever y'all were doing and left. The reason Killa didn't want to come is because Mina's sneaky ass was over there," she said as she laughed even harder. I had to laugh myself. Dozer was doing the most.

"Nikki, I just seen him and his new boo. Why is he checking for me?"

"I don't know, but whoever that nigga is, please get him home, because I ain't trying to be on that shit tonight," she said. We hung up laughing. I looked around my house and noticed my curtain was open, so Killa could've easily taken the pictures. This shit was crazy.

I decided to mess with his ass. I let Desmond spend the night. He slept on my couch. When I woke up, I had twenty messages and ten calls. Nikki, Mina, Riah, Dozer, and Fizz all called me. The messages were from Dozer. I didn't even read them. I deleted them all. I called them all back in the row that I loved them. Riah first, Mina, Nikki, Fizz, and Dozer was last, but he wasn't going to get a call from me.

Riah asked what everyone else asked. Who was the guy on the couch? Killa must've come back that night. Dozer needed to let that man have his private time. I went out, and Desmond was already gone. He left a note saying he caught a cab, and he enjoyed our night. The blanket he used was folded up. I thought about him again. Could it be?

Riah and I were at Roxy's house for lunch. We were meeting her new man she kept telling us about. Riah was on the defense, waiting for any sign that the man used drugs. I told her to give him a chance. We waited until he arrived. When the doorbell rang, Roxy came out the kitchen and answered it. We waited in the living room. When she came back, I think my mouth was open and eyes were big.

"Deacon James, this is my daughter, Riah, and my niece, De'Kiya. My son, you already met, and he is taking a nap.

"It is a pleasure to meet you girls. I have heard so much about you," he said.

"Nice to meet you," I said. Riah was in shock or something, because she didn't speak.

"Riah, are you okay?" Roxy asked.

"Oh, sorry. Hi, nice to meet you," Riah said.

Roxy cooked baked chicken, spaghetti, and salad on the side. I wasn't really hungry. The new birth control I started had me feeling nauseous. After the deacon blessed the food, I did manage to eat the salad and chicken. We all talked and got to know the deacon. I was all for Roxy meeting someone, but I never would've thought he was a deacon. Roxy said she told him about her past. He also told us about his past that led him to become a deacon. Roxy said she would be going to church with him more often.

#

I was at the shop doing Kiya's hair. I curled it real pretty for tonight. Riah was sitting next to us, waiting to get hers silk pressed. She wanted another middle part, because she said that's what Fizz liked. I was rocking a bob that was banging. I cleared my schedule, because I needed to get myself together for the welcome home party. Nazir was coming home today. Fizz and Killa went to get him while Dozer stayed back to make the party the best one yet.

"So what's up with you and Nazir," Riah asked. I decided to just tell them everything. I was beyond nervous to be face to face with him. I knew those bitches in the club were going to be all up on him.

After I finished their heads, we headed to the mall. I found the perfect dress. Kiya was also trying to shut some shit down. I told her Michelle was coming with Dozer, and she didn't seem pressed by it. I knew she was trying to make sure she out did the girl. I wasn't mad at her, though. I wasn't feeling that Michelle chick, anyway. She wanted Dozer for the fame. Fizz had picked out Riah's dress at first. I cursed his ass out, acting like she couldn't find her own damn clothes, but when Riah tried on the dress, I had to give him props. He had taste in clothing. It showed all of her curves.

We went back to my house and had girl talk. We called Mina, and she was on her way. Riah's ass stayed, asking questions about Nazir. She knew something. Fizz must've told her little ass something. I answered all of them, so she could shut her butt up.

"So if he wanted to get back together, would you take him back? Kiya asked.

"I really can't say right now. Nazir and I have so much history. I would've still been riding for him, until he consistently told me to move on. Finally, I did. Shit, I should blame his ass for pushing me to Mason," I said as I laughed. We laughed and chatted until Mina finally came. Once she got in, we all wondered what went down between her and Killa.

"Dang, y'all nosey," Mina said.

"Come with it. I know you got some juicy gossip," I said.

"Well, first off, Dozer is sprung as hell over you, Deedee... having my man come out late night to spy on your ass. Second, yes... I let him hit a home run, and boy did he hit it right. I can't be staying over there. I'll fuck around and get pregnant. We had sex four times that same night. He is so sweet. Under all that hardness, I found his soft side, and I know his real name," she said.

"Bitch, shut up! Did he really?" I asked.

"He did. I swear."

"What is it?" I asked, testing her.

"I'm not telling... starts with a T, though."

I knew she knew, and I was proud she didn't repeat it. Killa had found his match. Mina could be too much at times, but he needed someone to calm him. She seemed like the type to put his ass right in his place.

Fizz called, saying that they were back. He was taking Nazir to see Mom, and then they'd be at his crib getting ready.

We popped a few bottles. I took a shot to calm my nerves. We were all laughing, dancing, and singing. Nazir was on my mind, heavy. I didn't know what to expect once I saw him.

I told the girls I was going to bathe. I had two other bathrooms, so they all took turns getting ready. Mina was ready first, and she looked damn good. I told her Killa was going to kill her, because her ass was poking out. Riah came downstairs in her dress that I had already seen, but with her hair and makeup, she looked so beautiful, like a real queen. We were all beautiful, but Riah took the crown, hands down. Kiya came out, and I knew Dozer was going to be drooling over her. She was getting thick for her not to be having sex. It seemed like somebody was hitting it.

We were headed out the door when I got an unknown call. I didn't answer, because if you weren't registered in my phone with a name, you didn't deserve an answer.

"So, who's driving?" Mina asked.

"Riah!" Kiya and I said together.

"Really? Y'all lucky I love this car."

Kiya and I got in the back, giving Mina the front seat. Fizz called Riah, and I thought maybe I should have driven if he was going to keep calling her. My phone vibrated with a number I hadn't seen before. I decided to answer it.

"Hello!"

"Daddy is home. I'm going to see you tonight, right?" Nazir asked. Man, I wasn't trying to blush, and I was happy no one could see my face.

"Yeah, I'll be there. You know I wasn't going to miss your welcome home party," I said.

"That's what's up. See you in a lil' bit. You know your brother takes forever like a little bitch," Nazir said.

"Nigga, who you calling a bitch? Your ass the one just touching down. I need to see your player's card," I heard Fizz say.

"Oh, you gon' see it. Know that, nigga. Alright, sexy, see you later."

He hung up and I wondered if that was his number. I guess so, because he texted, saying store me in. I stored him in under Nazir.

"So that was Mr. Nazir, I take it?" Kiya asked.

"Yeah, that was him."

"Man, you need to quit playing, and get your man, girl. I hear it in your voice. You want him.

"I'll get my man only if you get yours," I said as I looked over at her.

"Touché," she said back. I knew I got her ass with that one. She needed to quit playing, though. Riah and Mina were the only ones happy and in a relationship while Kiya and I were playing, but I couldn't go backwards. I was only trying to move forward.

We drove around a bit more, because the two show stoppers in the front wanted their men to see them when they walked in. Shit, who knew how long that would be, because Fizz really did take all day to get dressed.

Kiya mentioned that she told her coworker, Desmond, to come. I asked her was she trying to get him killed, but when she mentioned that she thought he was gay, I laughed, hoping she was right. Fizz was finally in the club, so we headed in ourselves. We tried heading up to VIP, but niggas were on us. We finally made it up, and the DJ made a shout out to Naz.

"My boy, Naz, in the building tonight. All you single ladies make sure y'all welcome him home properly," he yelled, in the microphone. I didn't see him. I only saw Fizz, Dozer, and Killa. The guys noticed us when I noticed them. I saw the way they were looking. Fizz's ol' overly affectionate ass tongued Riah down. Killa hugged Mina, sitting her on his lap. I hugged Dozer and asked where Nazir was. He was too busy trying to look at Kiya. Kiya walked past him and sat next to Fizz and Riah. He watched her until she sat down.

"Bro, don't start, and I see your girl not here... which is a good thing."

"Man, where Nazir's ass go?" Fizz walked over and asked.

"Man, I don't know. He's probably with a bitch somewhere," Dozer answered back. Hearing that shit made me feel some type of way. I asked the ladies to come to the bar with me. Dozer said the hostess was bringing the drinks up. I told him they were taking too long. We made it down to the bar, ordered our drinks and headed back up.

"I see my friend, y'all. Heads up. I'll be over here," Kiya said.

"Bring him up, but I hope you're right about him being gay," I said. We headed up while she got her friend.

Riah

I was feeling myself tonight. By the time I turned twenty-one, I'd be partied out. That's for sure. We were heading back up to VIP when I saw my girl, Charm. She was with two other girls. I'm glad I ran into her. Now, we could all chill and party together.

"Mina, I see my friend, Charm—"

What I saw was one of her friends kiss Dozer, the other hug Killa, and Charm hugging on Fizz. Now, this club wasn't that damn dark for me to be seeing things. I put two and two together. She was talking about Fizz being the guy she met and really liked. Mina and Nikki peeped what I was looking at. I was damn near running to VIP with some heels on, at that.

I walked right up, but Charm was already on the elevator with her other friend. The one Dozer was with, I assumed, was his new girl.

"Why the fuck was Charm all over you?" I asked Fizz.

"Riah, I met her a while ago. She was cool people. I didn't know she was feeling me like that. I just told her I had a girl, and she left."

Mina was going in on Killa. He said he fucked her, but sent her on her merry way the next day. The girl with Dozer was asking what was going on. I walked off, about to confront Charm about her and Fizz. He had me fucked up.

"Man, chill out. I told you what just happened," he said as he grabbed me. He pulled me back to where we were sitting. I called her as soon as he turned his head. She was gon' tell me why the hell she was all over Fizz like that.

"Hello... hey, Charm. That nigga, Fizz, you were just talking to... come back down and see him real quick—"

He snatched the phone from me.

"Man... Charm, stay where you at. My girl tripping."

I slapped the dog shit out of him. How was he gon' get on my phone, telling her to stay where she was at? He acted like that was his sideline or some shit.

I noticed Charm coming over to us. I walked around Fizz so I could ask her what I needed to.

"Is there a problem, Riah?" she asked.

"Yes, this is my boyfriend, Fizz. I wanted to know what he is to you," I said.

"He's nothing to me. We kicked it a few times... nothing like that, though, but he never mentioned having a girl. I hope I didn't start anything.

"Nah, you good, but he's single now, so if you want to have him, go right ahead."

I walked off, and he tried calling me back. I didn't see Mina or Killa, so who knew what was going on with them. I went to the bathroom, because I been holding my urine forever. I noticed Deedee at the bar with her co-worker. He was actually cute. I was so pissed off that I didn't even feel like telling her what just happened.

I was walking into the stall when someone pushed me in. I was about to fuck their asses up. I turned around, and it was Fizz.

"Riah, she was cool—"

"Get the fuck out, Fizz!" I yelled.

"Can you just listen to me, please?" he begged.

"I have to use the bathroom."

He just stared at me, as if to say 'use it'. I did just that, because the liquor was running through me. I wiped and pulled my dressed down.

"Can you move?" I asked.

"Listen first. I was talking with her on the phone and texting. She told me she was a photographer. She's been to my paint shop, taking pictures of my work. Now, I admit it was a little flirting going on, and I should have stopped it, and mentioned I had a girl, but it was nothing," he said as he tried to pull me closer to him.

"So you out there spending time with bitches, flirting, texting, and calling, but I barely get a call or see you?" I asked as I looked at him. That shit hit straight to my heart. I never wanted to get that feeling again. I wasn't going to drop one tear.

"Riah, it's not like that. I love you and only you."

"Please... let me out."

When he opened the door, I washed my hands. People were staring, probably thinking we were crazy. I walked out, unbothered by his trifling ass. He followed me, and I kept walking until I found Deedee. She was still at the bar with her friend. I asked them to join me on the dance floor. I got out there and showed my ass. I was twerking on every nigga that came my way. The nigga that I was dancing with had fallen down. I turned around, and of course, it was because of Fizz.

"If you want me to turn this bitch out, I will, but you ain't about to disrespect me and think shit cool," he said, fuming.

"Fuck you! Go find your Charm, since she charmed your ass so much," I lashed out. I walked off and bumped into Mo and his boys. My eyes grew big. Why the hell would he come to this club out of all the clubs in Atlanta?

"Sup, Riah? You look beautiful," he said, He didn't even know Fizz was right behind me.

"I know damn well it isn't Mo mothafuckin' Summers!" Fizz yelled over the loud music. He did some hand signal in the air.

"Fizz, I know Riah has been telling you what I have been saying. I apologize for what happened. The day we met at Applebee's, I told her everything," he said. I was the one scared now. Why did he have to mention that?

"Applebee's? You been talking and meeting up with this nigga?" Fizz asked, as he pushed me, and I stumbled a little. I was pissed he put his hands on me which caused my reflexes to react on their own. I swung and hit him. The look in his eyes scared me. I didn't know if he was going to hit me back. I did hit him hard, so I knew he wanted to.

"Fizz, I swear if you hit my cousin, I will kill you," I heard Deedee yell. Dozer walked up and stepped in between us. I saw Nazir and Nikki walk up. Killa grabbed Mo, and some dummy that was with Mo tried to step up, but he backed down when Killa gave him that look. Killa tried pulling Fizz out the door. He kept trying to come at me.

"I know this bitch has lost her mind. She's been meeting with this nigga, so she's just as disloyal as he is," he said.

"Man, chill out! Take that shit upstairs to my camera room," Dozer said.

I walked away. Nikki grabbed my arm and asked what happened. I broke down right in front of her. She pulled me off the floor. Mina was asking what had happened. Deedee only told her what she saw. Nikki brought me up to Dozer's office. It was dark as hell in the hallway getting there. Once we made it in, the girls all started questioning me about what happened. I told them, and Nikki shook her head. She knew her brothers weren't shit. There was a knock on the door. Deedee got up and opened it.

"Can I help you?" she asked.

"Hi, I'm Michelle. Dozer told me to come in his office," she said.

"Well, go back and find Dozer. Tell him De'Kiya said you aren't welcome in this bitch," she said and slammed the door in her face. We all just looked at her.

Dozer

$\mathcal{I}$ did not picture the night turning out like this. I was trying to calm Fizz down. He wanted to kill Mo in my club which was a no-go. Nazir tried calming him down.

"I admitted I was wrong on my part with that Charm bitch, but her meeting up with this nigga? I knew it was something, because every time I brought his name up, she got so defensive. So you think that bitch can save your life?" he asked Mo.

"I told you what happened, so either you kill me, or let me go."

I knew Mo had heart. I couldn't say I agreed with what he did, but I can tell he was telling the truth about thinking it was a prank. It was Fizz's call on this, though. They talked back and forth, and finally, Fizz decided to let him go.

"Look… let him go, and stay away from Riah. Don't contact her again, or I'll send your bitch ass where the fuck you belong," Fizz said. Mo left, and we headed into my office. I bumped into Michelle coming out.

"Hey, you couldn't find my office?" I said and smiled at her.

"Yes, I did. Some girl named De'Kiya said I wasn't welcome. Maybe I should just go. This is your family's problems, so just call me when you leave here," she said.

"Yeah, okay. I'll see you later."

That bitch wanted to leave, so I let her. I walked into my office, about to curse Kiya out, but she wasn't in there. None of them were.

"Where the hell they go?" Nazir asked. We walked back down toward the floor.

"Look at their asses dancing like ain't shit happened," Fizz said as he looked down at Riah. We all looked down. I knew Nikki probably did that shit, preaching that 'never let a nigga see you sweat'. I saw Kiya and that same nigga on the dance floor. I followed her with my eyes as she walked over to the bar. I headed down, because she was due for a piece of my mind. Her back was turned from me. I sat right on the side of her, facing the dance floor.

"So you fucking that nigga?" I asked. She turned around so fast. I knew she didn't expect for me to approach her.

"You don't have the right to question me."

"I have every right. You were my bitch. Now you letting this square ass nigga hit. Shit, somebody hitting it. Your ass getting big, and your hips are spreading. You pregnant?

"You better go question that bitch, Michelle, because like I said, you don't have that right to question me," she replied.

"Oh yeah? Why you tell her she wasn't welcome. She can go wherever she likes, and you damn sure can't stop her," I yelled over the music.

"Look, my fault about that. I thought it wasn't her business to be involved in. If I knew y'all were that serious, I would've of let her come in," she said. I didn't know what to say. She was apologizing, so arguing with her was pointless. I just walked away. I loved that damn girl, and she wanted to be with that square nigga. I knew I needed to get my girl back. I walked back to VIP. Mina and Killa were all booed up.

"Where is Fizz?" I asked.

"He left… said he was going home," Naz answered.

Nikki and Riah walked up and said they were leaving. Nikki hugged me and Naz, and he whispered something in her ear. Riah didn't even look at me. I wasn't the one mad at her. Mina said she was going with Killa, so they left out right after Nikki and Riah. Naz and I chilled back while bitches came dancing all up on us. I looked down, and Kiya was still at the bar. I wondered why she didn't leave with her girls. I saw her dude walking up to her. He whispered something in her ear. She smiled, and they got up. They walked toward the door. I turned around, and Naz was right there.

"You staring at her, instead of taking her home with you? Let me find out you lost it."

"Man, it's easier said than done," I answered back.

"Shit, if it was me, my girl would be going home with me. Stop being so prideful, and make that shit work," he said. That's why he was my nigga. He didn't sugarcoat shit. He told it like it was. We decided to leave. I talked with the manager, and he assured me he had everything under control. Naz said he had something on the floor that he had to handle. I knew he was probably getting up with a bitch.

I had driven home, so that I could let Naz use one of my cars until we got his shit out of storage. I had a text from Michelle, asking if she could come suck my dick. I thought about her and Kiya. If I had to choose one, it would be Kiya.

Deedee

I just flat out ask Desmond was he gay. He looked at me funny for minute, and then asked how I knew. I told him because a bad bitch was in his presence, and he didn't even flinch. He came back to my house with me. We talked more, and he said he wasn't ready to come out and tell people.

"I'm glad you drove, because my people just straight left me," I said as I laughed.

"Right! Like, did they even say bye?" he asked as he laughed.

"Riah said something, but I wasn't listening. Dozer's ass had me watching that bitch he invited."

"Well, I'm going to get going, I have a little friend waiting on me," he said.

"What? Look at you! Well, let me walk you to the door," I said as I got up. The doorbell rang as soon as we made it to the door.

"Who the hell is that?" I asked like he knew.

He looked through the peep hole and smiled.

"What? Why you smiling? Who is it?" I asked.

"Your man," he said, as he opened the door.

"Dozer?"

"Kiya, I need to holler at you about something, and why is this nigga in your house?" he asked. I looked at Desmond.

"Call me tomorrow."

He hugged me and left. I walked away from the door. Dozer locked it and came in.

"What is it, Dozer?" I asked.

"I need you. I love you. I can't live without you. You mad about that shit with Riah. I told you I was sorry over and over. I was trying to protect you, but I get it. You wanted to be there."

"I'm over that. I loved you too, but things have changed. You've obviously moved on, and so have I."

"Tell me right now why you wouldn't pick me over him," he implied.

"Dozer, please stop this. I don't want you. Go to that Michelle bitch, or Kenda, or even Kim. Hell, they keep popping out the woodworks, anyway. You have options, so pick one," I said, hoping he would just leave. I was on the verge of crying.

"Once I walk out that door, it's over for good," he said.

"It's been over," I said. He looked at me and walked out of my house. Why couldn't I just say I loved him back and stopped this foolishness? Now, I let him leave for good.

I called Nikki and told her everything. She told me to just go to his house and tell him. I thought about it for a minute and decided I wanted him... all of him. I wanted him to have all of me. I showered, lotioned down in my new sheer butter body cream, and put on my sexy bra and panty set. I put on a long trench coat. It wasn't too hot out, but it wasn't cold.

I was so nervous, driving to his house. I needed to calm down. If not, I was sure to just turn back around. I prayed he was at home. I didn't see the car he usually drives in his drive-way. Before I gave up, I decided to just get out and see if he was there. I was outside ringing his doorbell. I was about to turn around when I heard him turning the locks.

"Kiya?" he asked, making sure it was me.

"He's gay."

"What? Who's gay?"

"The guy I've been with. He's gay. There's nothing going on with him and me. He's just a good friend."

"Okay, so what does that mean?" he asked.

"Can I come in?" I asked.

"No, I actually have company."

"Company? Oh! I'm sorry."

I walked off and heard him shut the door. I wasn't about to let no bitch take what was mine. I beat on the door, and he swung it open.

"Really, Kiya? What the hell is wrong with you?

"I love you too, Dozer. I want you, and I won't leave here until you say I can have you."

"I was just at your house. You didn't say any of this shit. Why wait until I leave and get all the way home?"

"Dozer, please just be patient with me. I want to be with you. I'm ready to give you all of me," I said as I pulled the coat opened.

"Damn—" he said.

"Dozer, why is she at your door step in her bra and panties?" Michelle asked, opening the door wider.

"Didn't I tell you that you weren't welcome? This is my man, and you got five minutes to get your shit and leave," I yelled.

She looked at Dozer for confirmation. He looked down. He knew what time it was.

"Dozer, really? You're going to let this trick just come—"

"Look, don't disrespect my girl. You heard what she said, so please get your shit and just leave," he said.

"You have to be fucking kidding me. You and this dumb bitch are crazy. I ain't going anywhere until I'm climaxing and calling your name," she said, looking at Dozer. Dozer seemed shocked she said that. I wasn't about to play with this fake weave wearing bitch. I walked over to her and hit her dead in her mouth. After that, I started drilling her. She tried fighting back, but I wasn't about to give her the upper hand.

"Chill, Kiya," he said, as he grabbed Michelle.

"Get the fuck out!" I yelled. She walked toward the living room with her lip bleeding. She gathered her things and walked toward the door. I knew she was hurt, but fuck her feelings.

"You think this shit over, bitch? You better watch your back," she said. Dozer walked over to her.

"You want to make it out of this house, don't you? Don't ever in your life make a threat to mine. That's the quickest way to end your life."

He grabbed her around her neck.

"Dozer, stop. Just let her go."

I didn't give two fucks about her, but I hated to see a man put his hands on a woman. I knew he was crazy like that, though. He pushed her out the door.

"Call a cab, bitch," he said, as he shut the door.

I looked out the window, seeing her on her phone. She started walking off. I saw her walk to the end of his long driveway. She waited a good ten minutes before a cab came. I laughed to myself.

"So right after you left my house, you went to pick her up?"

"Kiya, please. None of that shit matters."

He walked toward me and tried kissing me.

"You kissed her?" I asked.

"Didn't get the chance to. I had just gotten in before you got here."

We kissed long and hard. He tried taking me to the living room. They had a nice lil' set-up.

"So were you going to take her upstairs to your room?" I asked.

"You are the only woman who has ever seen my room, Kiya."

"Yeah… okay."

We made it upstairs. He looked at me and smiled.

"You came over here like that for me, huh?" he asked.

"You like it?"

"I love it, just like I love you."

After he said that, he grabbed and kissed me. He took my coat off me, and laid me back on the bed. We kissed, and he started touching all over me. I missed his touch so much.

"Please be gentle with me," I told him.

"You really ready for this?"

"Yes!" I told him. I saw his dick bulging, and I knew it was going to be painful. He removed the bra and panties I had on. He kissed my neck while I wrapped my arms around his.

"You are so beautiful, Kiya. I love you so much."

"I love you too, baby," I said and smiled.

*W*hen I opened the door to see Kiya on my door step, I knew we were meant to be together. She was so damn stubborn that she almost lost me. I picked Michelle up just to get Kiya off my mind. I never thought Kiya would've come with that sexy shit she was wearing. She looked so sexy. When she said she was ready to give me all of her, I wanted to take her right there in the doorway. I knew Michelle was hurt, but Kiya was who I wanted to be with.

I pulled her to the edge of my bed and started sucking on her pussy. I ate her like it was my last meal.

"Ahhh!" she moaned when I stuck my tongue deep inside of her. I played with her clit with my fingers as I flicked her with my tongue. Her moans got louder, and her legs started to shake.

"Ahhhh…Oh my God, I'm cumming," she screamed.

I got up and told her to move back to the center of the bed. She eased back, and I sat in between her legs, kissing her, letting her taste her own sweet juice.

"You know this is going to hurt, but I want you to know I love you, and I would never hurt you intentionally."

"I know," she gasped, still trying to catch her breath.

"Just relax, baby."

I kissed her lips again, sucked her nipples and put my finger inside of her. She was so wet and tight. I knew I was working with a monster. I prayed once I got started, she didn't stop me. I put on a condom, even though I didn't want to, when she told me I didn't have to. Since it was her, I didn't hesitate. If it had been any other female I would have strapped up.

I stuck the tip of my dick inside of her, and she started moving back. I smiled at her.

"Don't run from daddy, baby. You making it worse by tensing up. Just relax."

She finally let her body relax. I inched my way in, bit by bit. She was fucking my back up by scratching it. I finally got in enough for us both to enjoy. I was only giving her about eight inches.

"This hurts so much. Please go slow," she stuttered. I started stroking in and out of her while she was still tensing up a little.

"Come on, baby. Relax for daddy," I whispered in her ear.

"Sorry," she said. I felt her relax right underneath me. I kissed her while still stroking her wet pussy. I was stroking too good for my damn self. I tried my best not to bust yet, but damn that shit was feeling so good. I knew in a few weeks I was going to be knee deep in the pussy.

I noticed the expression on her face. She was starting to enjoy it.

"You like that?" I asked, still stroking.

"Ohhh my God, Dozer!"

I started to give her more inches, hearing her say my name.

"Ahhh…Yesss… Mmm…please, yes! Oh my!"

She couldn't even complete her sentences. I started to focus after seeing she was good.

"Damn, this pussy tight…this daddy's pussy, you hear me?"

"Ahhh…yes…it's yours!"

I started speeding up, causing her to really dig her nails into my back.

"Mmm, Do…zer," she managed to say.

"Say it, baby. Tell daddy?"

"I'm…I'm cumming…Ahh…shit."

"Damn…me too, baby…ahh this shit feels so good," I said, busting all in her shit. I stroked a few more times before pulling out of her. I wanted to bust another nut, but I knew she couldn't handle all of that.

"Wow, that felt…I don't even know how to describe it," she laughed and kissed me.

"You better tell that nigga to lose your number," I told her.

"Dozer, I told you that he's gay."

"I don't give a fuck. He still got a dick," I mentioned.

"I love you, and I am so sorry for how I was acting. Oh my God! I'm trying… still trying to catch my breath," she laughed.

"Don't give my pussy away, De'Kiya," I seriously voiced.

"Don't give my dick away," she snapped back.

"This your dick. As long as you take care of it, it ain't going nowhere."

I was serious about her not giving my pussy away. That pussy felt so tight and wet. I wanted to know how she was feeling. I hoped she knew the difference between me making love to her and someone raping her.

"You okay?"

"Yeah, I'm good. Like… that's the best feeling ever. I see why Riah be so horny," she joked.

"You crazy, but go make me a sandwich or something."

"No! I can't move my legs right now."

She laid down and closed her eyes.

"What? Man, you better not fall asleep. I know this dick got you weak, but damn," I told her, teasing her.

"Just give me ten minutes, and I'll get up.

It was now an hour, and she was knocked out. I should have told her when she woke up, her pussy would be sore.

I thought about Fizz and Riah. I knew he was mad, but I knew him. He probably was going in on her ass, still. I hoped he didn't do anything stupid. He had a bad temper.

I fixed myself something to eat and decided to lay next to my queen. I was tired as hell.

Nazir

$\mathcal{W}$hen I got out that crazy ass prison, Nikki was the first person I wanted to see. I saw her mother, and she asked if I was going to get back with Nikki. I had to hurry up and leave from over there. I knew Nikki didn't want anyone knowing about us, even though Fizz knew. When I saw her at the club, I wanted to snatch that dress off her and fuck the shit out of her. It was too much shit going on that I couldn't focus on just her. After Dozer dropped me off to get his car, I was going to head on over to her crib. I missed my baby, and the shit she had been going through was my fault. If I wouldn't have told her to move on, she would've never met that snake, Mason. Now, I had to fix her heart.

I was outside of her house. I rang the doorbell, and she looked out the window. She couldn't see my face because I was turned toward the opposite way. She opened the door, probably thinking it was Dozer, because she'd seen his car.

"What, Dozer—"

She saw my face once I quickly turned around.

"Nazir? What's umm… what's up?" she asked.

"Can I come in?"

"Yes, of course."

She moved out the way so that I could enter. Her home smelled so good. Fizz gave me her address. He said she upgraded, but he didn't say she was moving like this. My baby was doing well for herself. I looked at her as she led me to her couch. Her ass was even fatter. I wanted to grab it, but needed to see where her head was at first.

"Damn, you got this bitch decked out," I said, admiring her house.

"I try. It ain't nothing, though."

"Yes, it's something. It's nice. I'm proud of you, Nikki."

"You want a tour?" she asked. I was so focused on her lips that I didn't really hear her.

"What you say, baby?"

"I said do you want a tour?" she laughed.

"Yeah, sure. Let me see how you living up in this bitch," I said as I got off the couch and followed her. We went through the living and dining room. She showed me two rooms on the first floor and a bathroom. We went to the basement. It was furnished and decorated nicely. That was a whole other house down there with rooms and a bathroom.

"Where is your room? I asked.

She looked at me funny and headed back upstairs. I smacked her ass.

"Keep your hands to yourself, Nazir!"

"My fault. I couldn't help myself."

We got upstairs, and we headed up her staircase. I swear this was too much house for one person. We needed some little ones running around with all this space. Yeah, I had plans to get my girl back.

"This is my room," she pointed, breaking me from my thoughts. I looked around for a second. She was looking off in a different direction, so I made my move, catching her off guard. I grabbed her around her waist, kissing her neck.

"Nazir, stop," she said as she moved away from me.

"Why? You don't miss me?" I asked. She didn't answer me. I knew she did. I knew her better than she knew herself. I pulled her closer, kissing her. She didn't push me that time. I moved her closer toward the bed. I grabbed her ass.

"Take that shit off," I told her. She took off her dress. She was even more beautiful with her clothes off.

"Answer my question. Did you miss me?"

"You trying to talk or fuck?" she asked. That was my lil' freak. She was a lady in the street, but in those sheets, I knew she could handle her own.

"Oh, you know what I'm trying to do."

I took my clothes off as well. I slid right up in her pussy. Her shit was still tight and gripped my shit like I liked it.

"Damn, I missed you," I stated while sliding in and out of her pussy. Her juices were already flowing.

"Umm hmm, yeah," she moaned.

"Yeah, daddy remembered how you like it!"

"Ahh, yes! Right there, Nazir!"

I used to love that shit, hearing her call my name. It was still music to my ears. I let her get up, so she could get up on all fours.

"Yeah, assume that position for daddy."

She was throwing that pussy back on a nigga.

"Damn, Ma. Slow down," I groaned. She was about to have a nigga busting already.

"Mmm…just like that," she moaned when I started pumping faster in and out of her.

"That's what I want to hear, baby. Cum for me."

"I'mmm…"

"Me too, baby," I said as I busted fast, so I could hit that shit again. I was about to hit that shit all night.

I was downstairs on Nikki's couch when she came and joined me. I put her ass right to sleep after beating her pussy up all through the early morning. I wanted to ask her about some shit.

"So, you gon' tell me about that nigga, Mason?" I asked and stared at her.

"I really don't want to talk about that."

"Nikki, you know I blame myself for that shit, because if I didn't tell you to move on, you would have never been with him."

She didn't say anything. I knew she was in deep thought.

"What's up? Talk to me. You've been avoiding me while I was in prison… not writing me back!" I said.

"Nazir, I loved him. I gave him my heart, and he tried to kill my brother. I felt so stupid, because for the first time in a long time, I was happy."

"You loved him? Well, tell me this. Did you hesitate to kill him before you pulled the trigger?"

"No, I would never hesitate to pull a trigger when it comes to my brothers?" she said.

"What if I had a gun pointed at Fizz or Dozer and you walked in? Would you kill me?" I asked, wanting to prove a point.

"I mean… I probably would ask what was going on. I don't know. What does that have to do with anything?

"I just proved that you were not in love with that nigga. You were only in love with the idea of being loved."

She didn't respond, but just looked away. I knew that meant that she knew I was right. Prison did change me for the better. I was more observant. I read more, and I knew how to treat a woman. Nikki was a different breed. She wanted time and affection. She didn't care how much money a nigga had. That didn't impress her one bit.

"On some real shit, I want to give us another try," I mentioned.

"I think we…should maybe just be friends. That sneaking around, and—"

"Hold up! You the one that didn't want to tell your brothers. Fizz saw it and didn't trip, so what's really good?"

I was kind of pissed. She let me come in this bitch and beat that pussy up like she wanted a nigga back and shit.

"It's complicated."

"You making it complicated, so you telling me straight up that you don't want to be with a nigga?"

She sighed before speaking.

"It's not that I don't. I just need some time. You've been gone eight years, Nazir. I'm a different person from when you left. I view life differently. I'm trying to establish love and have a family."

"So you don't think I want all of that?" I asked, looking at her.

"You just got out. Enjoy yourself. I may not be the right one for you."

"I'm still not seeing the problem here. What I see is you trying to basically put it out there that you don't want to be with me anymore."

"You the one that told me to fucking move on!" she yelled.

"Okay, I didn't think you would go and fall in love," I voiced.

"Look, I don't want any bad vibes between us. I love you, and I think we should both just move on."

I shook my head up and down. Was I hurt? Yes, but I did tell her that shit, and it back fired.

"Well, I guess that's that, right? Thanks for the fuck. It was good."

I got up, got my shit, and left.

J wouldn't be a man if I didn't say I was pissed beyond measures with Riah. She was being disloyal by talking to that nigga behind my back. She wanted that hoe ass nigga alive. She could go be with that nigga for all I care. I didn't know if I was more upset that she lied, or if I felt hurt that she wanted that nigga alive for some reason.

I was headed upstairs to my room when I heard the door open and shut. I knew that bitch didn't bring her ass here. She was about to make me kill her ass. I walked back down the stairs and came face to face with her.

"Did you fuck her?" she asked.

"Fuck you mean?" I asked, pissed that she was looking so damn beautiful coming up in this bitch.

"Did you fuck Charm?" she asked.

"Man, get the fuck out of my house with that shit! Did you fuck that nigga, Mo?"

"Your house? Did you forget this is my house, too? And no… I didn't fuck him."

"You might as well had fucked him, the way you were riding his dick to save his life. Sneaking up, meeting with him… you a disloyal ass bitch, and I can't associate myself with a female like you," I yelled to her.

"You know what? I admit it was wrong for me to meet up with

him, but I did feel he didn't know what Chris was really doing. As far as being disloyal—"

She paused, and I saw a tear coming down her face. I felt something once I saw that, but I was pissed and had too much pride to acknowledge it.

"You're the one that's disloyal. You let that bitch, Charm, suck your dick. How I know? I called the bitch after the club, and she tried to play like y'all had this friendly relationship… like ain't shit go down between y'all, so we ended the conversation at that, but she called back. I answered, but come to find out, she accidently called. I heard everything… all about her sucking your dick at your paint shop, and you letting her take a picture of it, so don't come at me talking about being disloyal."

"Ray—"

"Don't Ray me. You were my knight in shining armor. Now, you're nothing but my enemy," she said and walked away. I walked upstairs because the look in her eyes said she was hurt. She said I was her knight in shining armor. Now, she hated me. I knew I fucked up and needed to fix it. I just didn't know how. I'd always been someone that could talk to people and make them feel better.

I was upstairs, and all of the sudden, I heard glass break.

"What the fuck?"

I jumped up, grabbed my gun, and ran downstairs.

"What the fuck is you doing, Riah?" I yelled as I watched her swing the bat in her hand at my shit in the house.

"You stood in the club and lied to my face," she yelled as she swung the bat at my TV.

"Riah, stop. Just leave if you don't want to be here. Why do this shit?"

She gave me the look of death, and then charged at me with the bat. I started moving backwards as she swung.

"Is you crazy?"

She swung again, and I moved just in time. I quickly grabbed her and took the bat.

"Let me the fuck go! I hate your lying ass."

"Riah, fuck it! I'll leave."

I got my phone and keys, and left. I called Dozer, but got his voicemail. I thought about going to Nikki's house, but I just decided to get a hotel.

In my room, I just thought about all the shit that went down. Riah was blowing up my phone, saying I was going over to that bitch, Charm's, house. I should ring Charm's fucking neck. I should've known she was that messy type. I never let her ass suck my dick. She tried a few times. She asked if she could take a picture of it, and I declined, so for her to pretend to call Riah back and say that shit was fucked up. I knew Riah wasn't going to believe me, so what was the point in trying to explain it. After I choked the fucking daylight out of Charm, she was gon' have to believe me then.

I tried closing my eyes, but I just couldn't stop thinking about Riah. She was ruthless with her mouth when she got mad. I felt like shit, but I knew there was no coming back from the shit I said. I shouldn't have started conversing with that bitch, Charm, in the first place. I had a major headache, so I decided I would call her and confront her about that shit tomorrow.

*I*t had been a month since I saw Fizz. He called, but I never answered. He left voicemails that I just deleted and left texts that I never opened. Everyone was saying just talk with him, but I was straight on him. I was working and going to school. I still stayed in the campus apartments. After that shit happened, I asked for an emergency transfer from the apartment I was sharing with Charm, but they informed me she had already left, so I stayed and asked them to change the locks. I asked if it was possible to pay the other portion so that I could live alone. The guy I was talking to said that since I was beautiful, he would mark that room as being full. He gave me his number, but I wasn't sure if I wanted to even use it. He was cute, though. He had a nice smile, dressed nice, and he had major jokes that kept me laughing.

I had decided to change my number. I called Deedee to give it to her, along with my mom and Joyce, of course. I loved Joyce, even though I hated her son. I wasn't about to throw our relationship we built away.

I had to get to class. Today, we were going over techniques and different ingredients used by different cultures all over the world. Last week, we talked about Italy and their food. I had been studying for our test next week, so my main goal was to stay focused. I was back driving my Honda, because I didn't want anything Fizz got for me.

I was just leaving class when I heard my name being called. It was the guy that worked in the office for the housing committee.

"Hey, Ronnie," I said, smiling.

"You done with classes for the day? Let's go grab something to eat," he said.

"Sure, but your treat, since you asking."

"Well, maybe next time," he laughed. We headed to a local burger joint. I was tired and still had to do some studying. All I did was go to school and work. I'd saved up so much money within those past weeks. The girl I was working for stayed giving me a bonus for working hard.

Ronnie and I were eating, joking, and having a good time. When I saw Nikki walk in, I tried to hide, but she saw me. She walked right up to me.

"Don't be hiding from me and dodging my calls, little girl," she smiled.

"I apologize. I just needed time to myself."

"Yeah, okay. I'll let you enjoy your lunch, but Fizz is on his way. He's meeting me here," she said and walked away. I hadn't seen him in a whole month. Why would he show up now? I told Ronnie it was time to go. He didn't ask why. He just said okay. We were walking out, and Fizz had just pulled up. I hurried and got in my car, and he jumped out of his.

"Damn, that's you?" he asked. I heard him because Ronnie took forever to get in the damn car. He thought Fizz was talking to him.

"It will be. I'm working on it," Ronnie said as he got in.

"Really? Why you tell him that? You have no idea who that is," I yelled.

"What I do?" he asked.

"Nothing, let me get you back."

I drove fast, trying to get him back to the campus.

"Who was that, and why are you driving so damn fast?" he asked.

"My ex," I confessed.

"Damn, my bad."

"It's not your fault. He's just crazy, and I don't want you to get involved with his crazy ass."

"Well thanks for telling me, but I'm not intimidated by anyone. I grew up in the hood, but I'm not about that life. I had goals, and I'm accomplishing them. My dad is the CEO of a fortune 500 company. He could buy me anything I want, but I'd rather work for it. I know the outcome of hard work, and I want to be just like him one day."

I looked over at him and smiled. He and I were definitely on the same level. I wanted to work my way to the top, also. There was no better feeling than doing it on your own.

"That's what's up," I managed to say.

"So… who was the girl that came up to you at the restaurant?" he asked.

"His sister," I answered.

"Oh okay! Well, since our date got cut short, how about I take you out this weekend?" he asked. I looked at him and thought why not. He was really a nice guy.

"We can do that, but it would have to be Friday, if possible, because I have a sleepover with my friend and cousin on Saturday."

"Friday is good. Maybe we can do a movie or dinner?"

"Let's do a movie, and how about I make dinner. I've been dying to cook some of the things I learned, but haven't had much of an appetite lately. Like, the only thing I really want is burgers," I said and laughed.

"Okay, that sounds cool. Just don't kill me," he added in a joking way.

"Boy, I can cook my ass off. Watch."

I dropped him back off to the campus and headed to my apartment. I decided to call Mina. Of course, she talked about Fizz and me. I changed the subject by asking her about Killa. She got all excited, saying he was everything she wanted, and that he was making her cum four or five times. She had me cracking up. She said she talked with Mo, and he'd been asking how I was doing. She said he never mentioned anything about what happened in the club. I guess he wasn't pressed about that shit. He was too busy being advertised on the TV. He'd been doing his thing in football.

I was cleaning the kitchen while still talking with Mina. We'd been on the phone for hours. She said she wasn't really feeling that law school shit, and she really wanted to be an interior designer. She most definitely could have been, because she was really good at décor and putting things together. She dressed very nice, and it wasn't even always name brand. She asked how I was doing again.

"Girl, I've been busy shit! I've been so fucking horny lately, though… like really horny," I said and laughed.

"Well, you're not getting dicked down. You're just missing your boo's dick. Why y'all won't just get back together. Y'all so stubborn for no reason at all."

"I'm straight. I told you I can't forgive that shit he did. He came at me all out of pocket about Mo, and he was the one getting his dick sucked," I said, getting pissed all over again.

"I think y'all should talk," she stated.

"No! I'm good. Can we stop talking about him? I'm just getting pissed off all over again."

"That's because you still love him," she expressed and said hold on. While I was waiting for her to return back on the phone, I thought about it. She was right. Shit, he was my first love, my everything, and he played me. I couldn't forgive him for that.

"Hello?"

"Yeah, I'm still here."

"Well I'll see you Saturday, right… at Deedee's?"

"Yes, and bring that 'I Never' game," I mentioned.

"Okay, I will. I'm about to get ready and go with Killa. Call me later."

After talking with Mina, I decided to study for my test some more. I grabbed my water and cheese dip I made. As soon as I sat down, my mouth watered, and I felt like I had to throw up. I ran to the bathroom and threw up. I decided to just lie down.

Dozer

I had just left the club for another meeting. We were having some All-Stars going down and someone came and asked could they have their party at my club. I asked their price, first. When he told me, I didn't even think to tell him mine. He was damn near double the price. I had to make sure shit was on point.

I pulled up to Fizz's house. He was getting in from having lunch with Nikki. I was pissed I couldn't make it, but duty called.

"What up, bro?" I asked, walking in.

"I pull up and she hurried and jumped her little ass in the car. On top of that, she had a nigga in the car with her!"

"Who?" I asked, wondering who the hell he was talking about.

"Riah! When sis and I went out for lunch, she was there. Nikki said she told her I was coming, so she hurried and tried to leave."

"Why didn't you just tell her the truth about that Charm bitch?" I asked.

"She ain't going to believe me. She heard the shit. It was made to seem like it was an accident, how Charm played it off."

"That bitch is crazy. You better handle that shit with Charm."

"I can't find the bitch. It's like she just disappeared. She changed her number and everything," he said.

"Damn, so what you plan on doing? You should at least try to talk to Riah."

"Bro, I have never been rejected by a bitch, ever in life, even if I did fuck over them. For Riah to just throw our shit away is fucking with me, heavily."

"We need to just take a break from everything... work and hustling. Let's go to Vegas again... or Miami," I mentioned.

"Yeah, that sounds nice. Set that up, bro."

"Nigga, what I look like... the host or some shit?" I laughed.

I kicked it at Fizz's crib for a while longer. Nazir was coming over and said he needed to talk with us both at the same time. I asked Fizz did he know what it was about. He said he didn't. I called Kiya and talked with her until he got there. I had been beating that pussy up left and right, and she was loving every minute of it. I wanted to ask her to move in with me, but every time I tried bringing it up, she had something to say about looking forward to seeing me sometimes. I didn't want to take that away. Absence does make the heart grow fonder. Kiya mentioned the girls having a girl's night at her house. I thought that would be the perfect opportunity for Fizz to get at Riah.

I was just hanging up with Kiya when Naz walked in.

"What up, nigga?" I asked.

"Man, shit... trying to decide if I'm going to go ahead and purchase that home or not?"

"You need to, because you can't keep staying in my shit," Fizz said and laughed as he came out of the kitchen, eating.

He was staying with me for a minute, but he started kicking it at

Fizz's crib, because he felt Kiya didn't feel comfortable with him around.

"Man, it ain't like you got a bitch living with you," Naz joked. We looked at Fizz, and he wasn't laughing.

"Too soon, mothafucka!" he said, and sat down. I looked at Naz, and we burst out laughing.

"Too soon to be joking that you don't have a bitch no more? Man, get your soft ass out of here. You done changed, man. That's for sure," Naz said.

"Whatever! That's still my baby, regardless," Fizz responded.

"This coming from the same nigga that was about to beat her ass in the club," Naz stated.

"Man, what your ass come over here to tell us, because you about to get put out," Fizz questioned as he laughed.

"Man, don't be threatening me, but on some real shit I want y'all sister, and—"

I had just taken a sip of my water when he said that shit. I spit that shit right out.

"Damn, nigga! You spiting shit on my floor. Maria, get in here and clean this up for me, before I put this nigga out," Fizz yelled, for Maria to come. She came right in.

"Go to basement so I clean in here," she said. She stayed putting people out her way. She didn't give a fuck. We went down to the basement.

"You playing, right? Nikki? What brought that on?" I asked.

Naz looked at Fizz, and Fizz looked at him. I wondered what the fuck they had going on. I hated when they did the sneaky shit.

"Bro, he's basically asking for your approval. He and Nikki was kicking it way back, right before he got knocked," Fizz confessed.

"What?

"I hope you ain't taking this the wrong way, but I love that girl, and she's saying we can't be together because she don't want us sneaking around, so you straight with that?" he asked.

"Wait... so you and Nikki? Man, get the fuck out of here. Y'all playing, right?"

"I took her virginity. That's mine for life," he said.

"Whoa! Whoa!" Fizz and I said at once.

"Ain't nobody trying to hear that shit. Now I don't have a problem with whatever y'all doing, but on some real shit, I don't want to hear anything about you fucking my sister, nigga," I roared.

He was my nigga, no doubt about it, but there were boundaries I had to set.

"I got you, but she been on some bullshit. I think she was really in love with that nigga, man. It's fucking with her on the low," he said.

"Well, you better hurry up and do what you need to... talking about that's your baby. Who sounds soft now, nigga?" Fizz laughed.

"Man, fuck you, but that's why I'm debating on this house. If we going to work, I could just live with her and pay the bills, or we could find one together, but y'all know how she is."

"Sure do, and good luck with that one, but I'm out. Oh yeah, I forgot to tell you, Fizz... The girls are having a girls' night at Kiya's, and your boo gon' be there," I said, putting him up on game.

"Straight! Oh hell yeah. I need y'all to crash that bitch with me," he got hyped and said.

"Shit, I'm with it. Maybe Nikki would stop running from a nigga," Naz laughed.

Deedee

*I*t was the night of our girls' night, and we decided to have it at Nikki's. Her house was the biggest. I had just left my house with my overnight bag. Dozer wanted me to sneak away after everyone fell asleep, and I was kind of thinking about it. Our first time was great, but the many times after that were even better. I wanted him to make me cum every chance we had. With him working and being in the streets. I had to make some pop ups and get it where I could. We fucked in his office, at the car wash, his club, and in the shower. Where ever we could. I wouldn't mind staying together and just being able to get it in every night, but he didn't bring it up, so I damn sure wasn't.

We had a long talk about everything. I brought up that Kim bitch that cleaned Fizz's house where Mason got shot. He told me again that he fucked her, but stopped after she started working for them. He said Michelle was someone who was to pass time until I got my act together. He mentioned he did like her, but she was too clingy which was odd, because he wanted me to be clingier to him. It felt good opening up to him, and him opening up to me. He asked did I have nightmares about Chris. I told him no which was the truth. He said I wasn't normal. At first, I thought I would have a hard time about it, but it never came to that, and I didn't think or dwell on it.

I had just made it to Nikki's when I saw everyone was there but me. As soon as I got in, I heard music and smelled food. Riah was cooking, of course. Nikki was making drinks, and Mina was twerking to some song. I laughed and smiled. I was happy with the bond we'd created with one another. Nikki was neutral between us and the guys. She only stepped in when needed or felt she was needed.

We were eating the chicken alfredo Riah made, and it was banging. I had seconds. Riah ate like a spoonful and said she didn't have an appetite. Maybe she was getting sick, or she was still stressing over Fizz. We all went around, talking about what we had going on and what men problems we were having. Mina and I were good. It was Nikki and Riah that did the most talking. Nikki really wanted to be with Nazir, especially after the night she had with him after the club. Riah only mentioned she was still hurt. She didn't say whether she wanted to fix things or not. Nikki told me what Fizz said about the Charm chick. Now, if it was me, I probably wouldn't believe it either, especially how Charm accidently said it over the phone. He had to figure that one out on his own.

"So, there is this one guy that has been so sweet and nice. He asked me on a date tomorrow," Riah gloated. We all looked at her. We didn't care, but if she thought Fizz was going to let that happen, she had another thing coming.

"Was it that cute guy you were at the Burger Joint with?" Nikki asked.

"Yes, that's him. He's really nice, sweet, and funny."

How she said it made me think maybe she was over Fizz.

"So what… are you giving up on Fizz?" Mina asked.

"Yes, y'all keep asking me that. The man cheated on me. Why wouldn't I?" I just broke down and told her what I heard really happened. The ball was in her court now.

"Really, so you trying to say he said Charm set that up? Well, if that's the case, why she didn't say she fucked him? Why say she sucked his dick?" She looked at us and asked.

"Maybe she wanted to make it seem believable," Mina mentioned.

"Well, I believe it, so I'm done and moving on… next subject."

We talked more when Mina said she had a confession to make. We all got quiet, wondering what it was.

"I was pregnant by Chris," she said and covered her face.

"Was?" Nikki asked.

"Yes, I got an abortion right before graduation. I'm happy I did, though, but I do think about it. I don't want to talk about it anymore, and please don't tell your men," she insisted.

I was about to say something when Nikki's doorbell rang like ten times. She grabbed her gun, and I grabbed mine. We heard the door come open, and I heard Dozer's voice.

"Where the party at?" he asked coming in. It was him, Fizz, Killa, and Nazir.

"Oh hell nah. It's girls' night. What y'all want?" Mina asked. Nikki didn't say anything. She just stared at Nazir.

"Yo, Kiya, let daddy holla at you for a minute," Dozer said, pulling me up from the floor where I was sitting.

"I heard Killa say the same thing to Mina as Dozer pulled me into Nikki's guest room.

"What's up, baby?" I asked.

"Nothing… just wanted to come and kiss you," he said as he kissed me. He rubbed my butt and laid me on the bed.

"Baby, you know I'm usually down, but there's other people out there, and I wouldn't want anyone hearing how you be screaming my name," I laughed.

"You got jokes, I see," he smirked.

"For real, I got you, later tonight."

I kissed him.

"The guys and I are flying to Vegas tonight," he uttered.

"Vegas?" I asked.

"Just to get away, clear our heads. Don't worry. I have something planned for us, soon."

"You better, and you better behave yourself. Matter of fact, I can't send you off all horny and shit."

"That's what I'm talking about," he smiled.

Nikki

$\mathcal{I}$ sat there, sipping my wine while Nazir stared me down. He was looking sexy as fuck. The wine wasn't helping either, because I wanted him to penetrate my pussy in the worst way. I looked over at Fizz, and he smirked at me.

"What's up, sis?" Fizz asked.

"Yeah, what's up, sis?" Nazir chimed in.

No his ass didn't call me sis like he just wasn't beating my pussy up a week ago. Yeah, that's right. Even after I told him I didn't want to be with him, I still let him slide through to fuck the shit out of me. He knew exactly where my G-spot was.

"That's funny," I eyed him.

"Riah, can I talk with you?" Fizz asked.

"Nope, you good," she snapped back.

"Come in here," he smirked as he walked off. I was hoping she stayed, so I wouldn't be alone with Nazir, because everyone else seemed to be occupying my other rooms. She got up and followed him. I couldn't wait to curse her out for leaving me.

"Y'all having a good time?" Nazir asked.

"Yeah! We were," I said and sneered.

"So you ain't now?" he said, as he stared into my eyes

"I didn't say that, but why y'all just barge up in my shit like that?"

"Because we can, but come here."

"Why?"

"Because I asked you to!" he demanded. I got up to see what he wanted. I knew what I wanted him to want, but that had to wait. Soon as I got close, he tongued me down, of course I had to open my mouth to let him. It felt so good kissing him. If I didn't have everyone in my house, he definitely would be hitting it right about now.

"I told them," he whispered.

"Told them what?" I inquired.

"I told your brothers about us… well, Dozer, because Fizz already knew."

"What did Dozer say?"

"He was shocked, but he gives his blessings."

"Blessing? You make it seem like we're getting married."

"I'm trying to get to that point, but you making it real hard for a nigga."

I looked at him and tried my hardest not to smile at that comment, but I failed miserably. Who was I playing? I loved this nigga, and would always love him. I pulled him upstairs because I wanted to talk with him, privately. I told him my fears and what I needed from him. I didn't need someone that was wining and dining. I needed more than that.

"You know I got you, Nikki. Don't ever question that. Just like back then… remember when you almost fell flat on your face when I first tried to holla at you?" he laughed.

"Yeah, and you caught me," I smiled.

"That's right… caught by a boss, and I've never wanted to let you go."

I hugged him and talked about other things. He told me they were flying out to Vegas tonight.

"Really? I wanted you to spend the night," I frowned.

"I just bet you do, freaky ass, but I'll get you right before I leave. That's a promise."

"You better. You bought that house yet?" I asked.

"Nope, I was hoping I got you back to ask you to move with me. You know I can cop something nice."

I did like my house, and I'd rather live here. I hated moving, anyway.

"Well, you could always just stay with me. I mean… if you want to."

"I can do that too, and take care of the bills. I got you."

He pulled me closer to him.

"Nazir, you don't—"

"Nikki, you know how I am. Let me be the man, okay?"

"Okay, baby, but you don't have to pay everything. We're going to be a team," I informed him. I thought about the money Mason left me. I didn't want to even mention that. I had already moved it. After getting it checked out, I deposited that shit in a hurry.

"You just can't help it. I got you, baby. Whatever you want to contribute, I guess," he said and grabbed my lip with his and kissed me. I couldn't wait until he was between my legs. I hoped everyone was occupied, because I wasn't about to control my moans.

Riah

I knew Deedee should have done girls' night at her house. Maybe Fizz wouldn't have felt so comfortable with coming in her house like he does Nikki's.

"Damn, your ass getting thicker," he replied.

"What can I help you with?" I asked.

"There's a few things I can think of," he smiled, showing those dimples. Damn, why was he showing out? He knew those damn dimples were my weakness.

"Look, what do you want?"

"You!"

"Well, that's not an option."

"There's so much I want to say, but I know you won't believe me, and it pains me to know that you don't know the truth."

"What truth?" I asked.

"About that Charm bitch. I never fucked her, and never let her suck my dick. I did flirt, and I admit that, but that was it," he disclosed.

"Fizz, it doesn't even matter anymore if you did or not. The fact that you thought it was cool to even continue to communicate with her even after you said she wanted to suck your dick—"

"You are absolutely right, and I can't take that shit back, but I can move forward and show you how much I am sorry."

192

"I can't, because in the back of my head, I'll always think you are doing something with a chick who's hanging around you."

"Really? If I can get past that shit with Mo, I know you can. When was the last time you seen that shrink?" he asked.

"I never saw a shrink. Dr. Acres is a therapist, and I don't see him anymore," I said, trying to avoid the whole Mo conversation all together.

"You need to, because you need him to help you figure some shit out," he joked.

"That is not funny, and I don't need to figure anything out. I'm super good."

"Oh, you super good? Well, let me get some super head."

"Fizz, get the fuck away from me," I said and walked away.

"Please let me get another chance. I love you, Riah with everything in me. I fucked up, and I want to make it right. I think we both made some bad choices. I forgave you, now forgive me, and move on with me."

He walked toward me, and I didn't move. I was still hurt. Why would he let that bitch suck his dick, and then think it was okay to come fuck me? I wanted to forgive him, but I couldn't. I was hurt. Then, how he clowned me in the club wasn't even cool.

"You remember how you clowned me in the club, pushed me, and called me a bitch? You're too much for me. I can't deal with all of that shit."

"You remember me seeing you at the burger joint with that square ass nigga?" he stepped to me and asked.

"What does that have to do with anything?" I asked.

"I'm saying I didn't bring it up, because it's in the past and irrelevant, so quit bringing that shit up. It's over and done with," he yelled.

"Why are you yelling, and he's not a square, first off."

"Please, don't do that. Don't defend the nigga in my presence."

"Well, if he's my nigga, then I'm gone defend him," I announced back.

"So that's you?" he asked, eyeing me like he was daring me to say yeah.

"Yes, that's all me," I said, licking my fingers. I knew that was a little too much, but I was trying to hurt him like he hurt me.

"Bitch, what the fuck is that supposed to mean. You fucking him?"

"See… you and that damn mouth. You so fucking disrespectful. How you gon' call me a bitch, because I'm defending my man. If you were man enough to keep your dick in your pants and not in that bitch's mouth, I wouldn't be defending another nigga."

I walked away, but not fast enough, because he grabbed my arm.

"You better not be giving my pussy away. That's gon' always be my pussy," he grabbed me by my hair and whispered in my ear.

"This ain't never going to be your pussy again!" I stepped to him.

"Oh you think I'm playing don't you?"

He picked me up and carried me to Nikki's basement. I tried to squirm out of his arms, but he was too strong.

We made it to the basement, and he pulled me into a room and locked the door.

"Really? Open the door, Fizz!"

"Nah, not until I get some of my pussy."

"Is you crazy? I am not about to cheat on my man," I said, lying, hoping he would let me out.

He was walking toward me. I wasn't scared of him. I was scared that I would give in. He tried kissing me, but I turned my head. He started kissing and sucking the hell out my neck. I knew there was probably a hickey there. Him sucking on my neck had my juices flowing. I was horny as fuck. He put his hand inside of my pajama pants I had on and inserted his fingers in my juice box. I swear I didn't mean to moan.

"Ahhh...stop...please, stop," I said.

He pulled my pants all the way down and pulled his dick out. He slid in, moaning while entering me. I missed that feeling so much. He was pumping in and out with my legs over his shoulders.

"Damn, your shit wet as hell, he moaned.

"Fizz, oh my God! Right there... please don't stop."

Just a minute ago, I was saying stop. Now, I was telling him don't stop. This shit was crazy. He knew what the fuck he was doing. I hated and loved him at the same time.

"Right there…God damn, I'm about to bust," Killa said. He had sucked me so good, I wanted to return the favor.

"Damn, baby. You the truth," he said. I kissed him and got up. I knew just how to get him right.

"Damn, girl. You making a nigga not want to leave," he blurted.

"Leave where?" I raised my eye brows.

"The fellows and I are going to Vegas tonight."

"Vegas?"

"Yes, baby. You straight with that, right?"

"Well, I guess I have no choice, since I'm just now hearing about it."

"Aww, don't be mad, baby. You know once I get back, I'm all yours?"

"Oh really, because it seems like you're Fizz and Dozer's.

"Mina, really? They are my bosses. I'm always on the clock. I can't just not answer when they call or give me a job," he said as he rubbed my face.

"Whatever! It's nothing against them, but sometimes, I want to have you to myself one full day," I voiced.

"Aww, baby, well when I get back, I promise to spend some quality interrupted time with you, okay lil' mama?"

"I guess!" I smiled and kissed him.

"So did you talk to your parents yet?" he asked.

"No I didn't. They were home for a day and left again. My father has a case out of town, and my mom went to assist him," I said.

"So are you going to tell them you don't want to continue to go to law school?"

"I thought about it. Maybe I should just go and maybe somewhere down the line I can do what I really wanted."

"Lil' mama, don't do what someone else wants you to do. You'll never enjoy it," he mentioned and pulled my chin up to look at him.

"You're right, and it's not that I don't like it or think I'll be good at it, because I would make a wonderful lawyer, but it's not my passion. I don't get excited talking about it like they were."

"Well, do what's best for you, because ten years from now, I don't want to hear you saying you trying to go back to school," he laughed.

"You plan to be with me ten years from now?" I asked while watching his eyes.

"Of course, and have some little mamas running around."

My heart skipped a beat when he said that. It probably was going to be a girl, but I killed it.

"Wow… okay, daddy. I see you," I said, trying to hide the pain I felt inside. We laughed and hugged. I was happy I met Killa. He was someone I could grow with. He talked about opening a tattoo shop, and he got licensed years ago, but never did it. I hoped to encourage him to do so.

"I hope Nikki won't be mad. I feel bad now, sneaking off."

"Nah, sis ain't tripping. Plus, she's occupied right now. Everyone is."

"How you know?" I asked curiously.

"Because I do. Now, let's go and see who all is done fucking."

I laughed as we went to find everyone else. Deedee and Dozer were in the living room hugged up.

"Them nigga's still knee deep in some pussy, I see," Killa said to Dozer.

"Hell yeah. We got to bounce soon. Flight leaves in two hours," Dozer expressed. We chatted until Riah walked in, grabbed her stuff, and walked out the door. I looked at Fizz like what the fuck.

"What you do to my cousin, Fizz?" Deedee asked.

"Shut her ass up. She'll be alright. She just in her feelings right now."

"Damn, you stay running her away," Killa said, and we all laughed.

"Man, fuck you. Y'all ready? Where Naz's ass at?" Fizz asked.

"Right here. Let's roll," he said, coming from upstairs. They left, and I just looked at Deedee like what the fuck was going on. Nikki was upstairs, and Riah just left. I called her phone, and she said just tell her when he was gone. She was referring to Fizz. I told her they left because they had a flight to catch.

"A flight? To where?"

"Vegas… didn't Fizz tell you?"

"Hell nah, he was too busy fucking me. He ain't tell me shit," she said.

"Girl, yeah. I was pissed, too, but it is what it is."

"I'm not tripping. He ain't my man. Fuck him."

"Wait... didn't you just say he fucked you? How is it fuck him now?" I asked.

"Long story... I'll tell y'all when I get back. I'm turning around now."

I couldn't wait until she got back. I called Nikki down. Her ass was glowing.

"Y'all bitches get a little dick and don't know how to act," I blurted out.

"Bitch, who? I know how to act. I got too much dick to be honest," Nikki said.

Once Riah made it back, we all talked about what happened. One thing we knew was that we all got fucked and left. We laughed and just laid around. I texted Killa all types of kissy faces. I hadn't been on my Instagram in a while, so I got on there. I looked at my profile and saw Chris and I pictures. I deleted all of that shit. I added pictures of Riah and myself. After that, I got off and decided to go to sleep on them, because I was tired.

I was just pulling up to my mom's to get Rico and take him out for ice cream. It was hot today, so I wore a nice lil' sun dress. I walked inside my mom's house, and he ran and hugged me.

"Can I get ice cream and pizza?" he asked.

"Yes, I guess," I told him. My mom came out. She was looking very beautiful herself. I was happy she was going to church and staying on the right path. Deacon James was exactly what she needed.

"Hey, baby. Thanks for coming to get your brother. That's all he talks about is my Riah this and my Riah that. I told him—"

"You told him what, mama? What's wrong?"

"Rico, go in your room real quick. Let me talk to your sister."

He ran in his room and shut his door.

"Riah, are you pregnant?"

"What? No, what made you ask that?"

"Because your hips spreading, face getting fatter, and your titties getting bigger. I'm going to ask you again. Are you pregnant?"

"Mama, honestly… I don't know. I haven't had my period. I've been throwing up, and have little to no appetite on some days," I confessed.

"Lord, child. Take Rico on y'all little outing. I'm going to evening service with the deacon, but when I get back, I'm bringing a pregnancy test back."

"Okay," I said.

I was scared now. I thought if I just kept putting it off, I would eventually get better or my period would magically appear. I wondered if this was how Mina felt when she found out she was pregnant.

I took Rico out for pizza first, and then ice cream. I took him to the park and let him play. He was playing ball with some of the kids. I started thinking about Ronnie. We were going on a date later, and I had to admit I was excited. He was someone I looked forward in talking to, but if I was pregnant, that meant that Fizz was the father. I immediately stopped thinking about that and told Rico it was time to go. I still had to prepare the meal I wanted to make for Ronnie.

I asked him about mom, and he didn't have one thing bad to say about her. I was happy about that. I looked at him and told him to come on so we could go.

"Riah, can you come get me next week and take me for ice cream," he asked.

"I don't know. Mom mentioned you hit a boy at the park the other day. You can't just be hitting people," I told him.

"Well he took my ball, and I told him to give it back twice, and he didn't," he confirmed.

"Well, do you think it was a better solution than hitting him?"

"Nope!"

"Boy! Yeah, I don't know about ice cream next week. Get your temper under control, and I'll think about it."

"Ugh, okay," he whined.

"You ready for school to start back?"

"No, not really because I like staying up late playing my video game."

I just shook my head. I was about to hurry up and drop him off. I made it to my mom's, and she was standing in the kitchen, waiting. I knew she wasn't going to let this go. Rico washed his hands and ran into his room.

"It's in the bathroom. Read the instructions and come out when you're done."

Damn, did she have to sound like a mama? I know I was only eighteen, but she acted like I was twelve.

I went into the bathroom, read the directions and peed on the stick. I waited for the results. I sat there for ten minutes, not wanting to look. My mom asked was I okay, and I told her no. She opened the door, read the results, and hugged me.

"It's going to be okay, Riah. We will get through this."

So did that mean I was pregnant? I grabbed the test from her, and sure enough, I was pregnant. How could I let that happen? It was too late to be asking that.

"Mom, I'm not keeping it!"

"The hell you is! Ain't no abortions in this family. Fizz would be there to help you, and you have me. I'll help you along the way. I looked at her and started crying.

"What about school?" I asked.

"Riah, you act like you're going to be disabled. You can still go to school and become a chef. Now, you need to talk with Fizz about this. Deedee and Mina told me y'all broke up, but he has the right to know."

I knew she was right, but I wasn't ready to tell him that yet. I stayed around for a little while longer. I headed home after I thought about my date. I called Ronnie and was about to cancel, but he had me cracking up, forgetting all my problems. Ronnie and I were at the movies seeing *Underworld: Blood Wars*. He was all into the movie. I would have been, if I wouldn't have gotten the news I got earlier.

"You okay?" he leaned over and asked.

"Yeah, I'm okay."

We continued to watch the movie. He put his arm around me and I didn't mind it one bit. I was glad Fizz was in Vegas, because he always seemed to pop up out of nowhere. After the movie, we went back to my apartment. I fixed our plates, and poured us up some tea.

"Okay, this is my Italian sausage recipe," I said. I had it so pretty that it looked too good to eat.

"Damn, this looks too good to eat," he mentioned.

"I know, right. That's what I said."

I watched him take a bite and watched his facial expression.

"This is on point. You know Italian food is my favorite, right?" he asked.

"I know. That's why I wanted to surprise you."

"That's what's up. I really appreciate this."

We ate, talked, and played spades. Well, he basically was teaching me, because I didn't know how to play. He kept staring at me, and I wondered what he was thinking.

"Do you like me, Riah?" he asked.

"I do. You're a nice guy."

"Okay," was all he said.

"So, do you like me?" I asked.

"Yes… a lot. You're so beautiful. All I can think about is kissing you," he confessed to me.

"Wow, I don't know what to say. I mean I like you too, but—"

He got up, walked over to me, and kissed me. I didn't stop him. He pulled away, and I still had my eyes closed.

"I hope I didn't overstep my boundaries?"

"No, you didn't. I enjoyed it, actually."

He smiled and kissed me again. I didn't want it to go any further. I was carrying someone else's baby. What would I look like fucking him.

"I'm not really ready for all that yet," I said, looking down.

"No pressure, beautiful. I better get going, though."

"Okay… I'll call you."

"Yes, now, I'll have to cook for you, or at least try," he laughed.

"Umm, just leave the cooking to me."

"Yeah, let's do that. Do you mind if I take some home," he asked, pointing to the food.

"No, let me get you a Tupperware to put it in. I gave him majority of it, because I wasn't going to eat any more. I wasn't really feeling that good. After he left, I made up in my mind that I was going to go MIA for a while. I just needed to focus on me… not from him, but mainly my family, and Fizz.

*I*t had been over three weeks, and I hadn't seen Riah since I fucked her that night. I couldn't even enjoy myself in Vegas because she was on my mind. I talked with Kiya, Mina, and Nikki, and they all said she called and text, but they hadn't seen her in while. I called my mom, talking with her, and she mentioned Riah came to visit her. That wasn't shocking. Everyone loved my mom, so I knew Riah would to. I told Killa to get her number from Mina's phone. I knew he didn't want to, but he felt my pain. I called her, and she didn't answer. She knew my number by heart. I waited and tried again, but still no answer. I thought about going to her apartment, but didn't want to intruded on her new roommate. She told Kiya that Charm moved out and she was possibly going to get another roommate. I still hadn't seen or heard from Charm.

I had just left the Recreation Center, headed to Nikki's shop. I didn't call, but she knew what day it was.

"Girl, that's your fine brother?" I heard some chick say when I walked in.

"Yeah, that's him," Nikki said.

"How long you gon' be?" I asked.

"I can do you right after this wash," she answered.

"Cool, where your girl been hiding?" I asked, referring to Riah.

"Shit, who you asking, I haven't seen her little butt in a while either. She called, and checked on me. That was about it.

"So do you have a girl?" some chick next to me asked.

"Yeah, I do."

I hated when those hoes were all over me when I walked in Nikki's shop. Nikki got me in the chair, and I started talking about Riah. I told her how much I missed her, and how I wanted her in my life. I needed to find that Charm bitch. I didn't want to take it there, but she was about to get hurt, fucking with me.

I hit Sir up and told him to meet me at the spot. I gave him the information needed on Charm. I called Roxy next. I told her about what happened, and she told me that Riah had always been stubborn and held a grudge. She told me to just keep trying and not to give up on her baby.

I started sending flowers to her apartment, and she never responded to them. I sent her a necklace, and she didn't call to say she liked it. I finally just went to her apartment, and she wasn't there. I was just over it. I didn't have the energy to chase her anymore. I didn't want to put Sir on her also, but I just needed to see her. I needed one more chance to get at her. I called him up, and he laughed, saying I had hoe problems. It did seem that way.

I was going into my house when Sir was calling. I hoped he had some good news for me, because I was about to say fuck it and Riah, too.

"What up, Sir?"

"I'm following that Charm chick now. She's at the zoo, taking pictures… seems like of random things," he stated.

"Damn, that's a little ways from me. I'm on my way though. Don't lose that bitch," I added. I called Nikki, because I needed her help on this one. As always, she was down to ride.

We had finally made it to the zoo. I called Sir, and he directed me right where she was. Nikki and I got out and walked right up behind her. She was too busy taking pictures. She wasn't paying attention to her surroundings. I decided to give her the perfect picture by walking directly in front of a red bird she was trying to capture.

"I see you out capturing moments," I interrupted.

"Fizz, oh my God! I haven't seen you in—"

"Charm, don't fucking play games with me. Why you pull that slick shit and call Riah with that shit."

"With what? I didn't call Riah... about anything. Last time I talked with her was after the club," she stuttered.

"So you gon' keep lying?"

I stepped toward her and she step back, bumping into Nikki.

She turned around, and her eyes got wide. Nikki's presence alone could shut down any bitch.

"See, bitch... what you're not going to do is play like my brother is stupid. I'm gon' need you to boss up and tell him the truth. My patience with bitches like you are slim to none, so to save you an ass whooping, you better speak some truth into existence like now," she threatened.

"Look, I was just mad that she tried coming at me like that, and a little jealous that you were her man. I didn't mean to start anything... really."

Bitches killed me, always talking about they didn't mean to start anything, but this bitch clearly took it overboard.

"You sound fucking stupid, you a dumb ass bitch. I'm gon' let you have that one though."

I walked away. I was recording the whole thing. I would let Riah listen to it, in hopes that she'll know that the crazy bitch was lying. Nikki just had to mess with her by knocking her camera out her hand. She didn't even pretend to be tough. I laughed, and we walked away.

I dropped Nikki off and headed home once again. I looked at the car I bought Riah and smiled. She was so happy that day. I hated I fucked that up. I should've never been entertaining that bitch in the first place. I opened the door and could smell her scent. I wanted my baby back. She was my calm and kept me level. She was so funny and cool. I looked down at my vibrating phone. It was Sir again.

"Sup?" I asked.

"She's at Ruth's Chris Steak House downtown, the sexy one," he said as he laughed and hung up. I was going to kick his ass, admiring my woman and shit. I grabbed my keys and headed for Ruth's. I was sure going to send him a bonus. He was working overtime for a nigga. He caught two bitches in the same day.

I was pissed. Traffic was so heavy. Being that it was Friday, I should have known. I hoped she was still there when I got there. I was turning into Ruth's parking lot when I saw her driving off with that same nigga. I drove her car just so she could see that shit. I wasn't sure if she saw me or not, but I wasn't tripping. She wanted to be with that nigga. Fuck him and her.

Deedee

I was just getting in from work. I thanked God for Desmond every day. He was a blessing in disguise. My work load had been manageable. Dozer was on his way to pick me up. I was spending the whole weekend with him. I was so excited to have some alone time with my baby. I was putting my sexy lingerie in my overnight bag when my phone started going off.

"Hey, Riah!"

"Who you around?" she asked.

"No one, yet. Dozer is on his way. Why, what's wrong?"

"Deedee, when I tell you this, promise you won't tell anyone... not even Dozer."

"I won't! Tell me."

"I'm pregnant... like maybe almost three months."

"What, by Fizz? OMG! Does he know? Well if you're telling me not to tell anyone, I guess not. Wow, Riah! Are you okay?"

"Yes, your auntie is the one who told me. She knew just by looking at me."

"Damn…that's crazy, but please tell me you are going to tell Fizz."

"Yeah, when the time is right."

"There's never going to be a good time, so just tell him. He's been calling around, looking for you, and coming to your apartment."

"He came to my apartment? When?"

"Just the other day," I mentioned.

"Wow... yeah, I need to move."

"What? Why are you hiding from that man, Riah? He loves you."

"No he doesn't, or he wouldn't have done what he did."

She sounded like she truly believed he let that girl suck his dick, even when I told her what he said. She was so stubborn. I chatted with her a bit more. She promised to come see me Sunday evening, because I was going over Joyce's with everyone else for dinner... everyone except for her.

Dozer called and said he was outside, but he was coming in. I thought he was on some freaky shit, but his face said differently.

"What? What's wrong?"

"Kiya, when I tell you this, don't panic."

"That makes me panic, just by you saying that. Tell me!"

"Your tires are on flat."

"What? I probably ran over something," I said, wondering why he looked so concerned.

"All four are slashed," he uttered.

"What?"

"Somebody had to slash them. You just got here what... an hour ago? They recently did it."

"Wow! Are you fucking kidding me? So you got bitches fucking with my car?"

"Wait, how you know it's somebody I know? It's probably that faggot you work with."

"Why the hell would he do that?"

"Why it has to be somebody I know?" he asked.

"I'm just tired of this shit, like really! What else could happen?"

"Look… I'll go tomorrow morning and get you a brand new car. Put it in your garage for now. I don't know why you don't use your garage anyway," he said.

"I just need tires, not a new car. That doesn't make any sense. I swear y'all just throw money away."

He didn't pay me any mind. I watched him drive my car into the garage, making all types of noise. He came out, we locked up, and he said he was going to put his people to watch my house. That made me feel a little better. I thought it could be that bitch, Michelle, or Kenda. I didn't know which one was crazier.

We made it to his house, and he ran me a bath. He had the biggest tub, and I just loved taking baths there. I undressed from my work clothes, and he helped me in. He had me feeling like a true queen.

We talked about my car, and I got him to only get me tires. A brand new car wasn't necessary.

"You are just too beautiful. You know that?" he asked.

"Thank you. I love you so much. You really have been taking good care of me."

"I plan to do a lot for you, but I wanted to talk to you about something," he said, as he sat on the edge of the tub.

"Okay, what's up?"

I wondered what he was gon' say. I hoped it wasn't bad news.

"I love you so much, I know some days we can't see each other, but what if we stayed together… that way, every night I can lay with my queen and wake up to your beautiful face."

I smiled and blushed. That's exactly what I wanted to hear. I was saying yes in my head, but couldn't get it out.

"Hello? Did you hear me?" he asked.

"Sorry, but I've been waiting for you to ask me."

"Really, and here I was thinking you wouldn't want to," he expressed.

"Get in with me," I told him. He got in, and of course we had a little fun. I wasn't thinking about what happened to my car.

Nazir

I told Nikki I wanted to take her out tonight. She said she wouldn't be done with her last head until about nine-thirty, and she still needed to come home, shower, and find something to wear. She asked where we were going. I told her to a romantic dinner, walk in the park, and back home so I could fuck her lights out. She told me to pick her out something to wear. I had just bathed myself and finished unpacking all my shit in the walk-in closet she gave me. I had a few hours still before she got home.

I was talking with Fizz, and he sounded so depressed. I almost invited him out with us. I told him to try at ol' girl one more time, and if she didn't come around, then fuck it. I didn't tell him to give up, because when it came to Nikki, I didn't. I knew how that shit felt, and it didn't feel good, watching someone you love slip away.

I put everything back in place, and broke down the boxes that had all my things in before I put them away. Nikki said Maria could help, but I didn't need her. I always knew Nikki would be my wife, and I planned to make that happen soon. One thing about me was that I had more money then I knew what to do with. My shit was tucked away while I was in prison, thanks to Dozer and Fizz. Those niggas were my brothers. When I got locked up, they told me not to worry about shit. I came home to everything but that house I told them to sell. I know Nikki didn't want a man just lying around the house, so I decided I was going to start my workout gym. Right before I went in,

I was just in the midst of opening up a gym. I did some research, and mothers were paying thousands of dollars for trainers to get them in shape. I could do that shit, and help some gain the confidence they needed. I mentioned it to Nikki, and she said she didn't want young, or old women around me. I told her she didn't have shit to worry about. She knew where my heart belonged.

My phone rang, breaking me from my thoughts.

"Sup sexy?" I answered.

"Did you find me something to wear yet, or are you just playing around, wasting time?" she asked. I laughed, because I hadn't found nothing yet.

"My bad, baby. I'm about to right now. It'll be on your bed when you get home. I hung up with her, walked into her closet, and looked through her dresses. I found a red and black one I thought would looked sexy on her. I looked around for shoes that would look nice, and my eye spotted a bag. It wasn't a bag for a female, but more for a male. I tried turning around and forgetting it, but I couldn't. I walked over to it and opened it. I saw an envelope with Nikki's name on it. I opened it and read it.

I was waiting for Nikki to get home. What I read had me pissed the fuck off. Not only was she sitting on $600,000 that he left, but she wore that damn ring he gave her. I heard her coming upstairs. She was smiling like she didn't have a care in the world.

"Hey, baby. I thought you said my clothes would be out?"

I walked over to her and snatched that ring off her finger. She looked at me like I was crazy.

"What the fuck is your problem?" she asked.

"So you walking around this bitch with a dead man's ring on, and sitting on $600,000?"

"Did you go through my stuff?"

"That's beside the fucking point! I read that letter. You can't be serious, Nikki!"

"What you mean, I can't be serious? You think you are the only one that ever loved me?"

"That's not what I'm saying, but that shit is fucking crazy. You don't see how fucked up that is?"

She threw the ring at me walked in the bathroom, slamming the door. Now, she was pissed. I should be the one pissed. Why the fuck was she holding on to that letter like it was some precious cargo?

"Nikki, open the door!" I yelled.

"Just leave, Nazir. I don't have time for this shit. If you're going to act all insecure over a dead man, then just get the fuck out."

I couldn't believe she said that. I wasn't insecure about shit. I was leaving though, because I was becoming real pissed and didn't want to be around her ass at that moment.

Riah

I had been throwing up all day since the crack of dawn. I was beyond tired of that shit. Ronnie asked me to come chill with him. I told him if I was feeling better, I would. I was finally able to keep the crackers I'd been eating down. I showered, got dressed, and headed to his spot. I had to work today, so I needed to get up and moving anyway.

Once I made it to his house, I called and said I was outside. He had a nice lil spot. I'm sure his dad bought it.

"Hey, beautiful. Feeling better?" he asked.

"Much better. How was your day?"

"It was straight. Some chick come in the office and was demanding to transfer. I asked her for a reason. She said she saw an ant crawling. I told her, girl this the south. You better get used to it. She didn't say ants. She said one fucking ant."

I laughed, and we decided to take a walk. I was a little tired, but it was needed for me.

We walked and just talked about everything. He lives right down the street from a park. He grabbed my hand, and we walked hand and hand.

"What's your favorite color?" he asked me.

"Umm, I don't have one anymore, because I like all types of colors now. Whatever looks good on me, I guess."

"Well, that dress looks very nice on you," he expressed.

"Thank you," I said as I blushed. He was acting really weird. I don't know. Something was off with him today.

"What's wrong with you?" I finally asked.

"Nothing, why?"

"You're acting weird," I replied.

"That's because I have something to ask you, and I don't know how you're going to react or what you're going to say."

"Well, just ask me."

I prayed he didn't ask was I pregnant. Once my mom pointed out that my breast were getting big, I started to notice it myself.

"Do you want to be my girl?"

I wasn't expecting that. I liked what we were. I didn't want a title on it, though. I mean, I was pregnant. Damn, I knew I had to tell him now. We came along to some benches. I stopped and sat down. He followed suit.

"Ronnie, I'm pregnant!"

I held my breath when I told him that.

"Damn, already? All we did was kiss," he said in joking way. It was just like him to turn an awkward situation around.

"Is it by your ex?" he asked.

"Yes, and he doesn't know yet?"

"Well you should tell him. How long have you known?

"About a month now."

"Riah you should tell him. If it was me I would really want to know."

"I know, and I will, but I don't think I could be your girlfriend until I figure all that out."

"Well the offer will still be out there, whatever you decide."

I didn't know why this man came into my life, but it had to be for a reason. We kissed and headed back to his place. As soon as we got back, I threw up. I told him I was going home to lay down. I had to work and couldn't keep shit down. I was still going to go, though.

I walked into work, feeling like death. I put my purse in my office and headed to the front. I checked the labels that were just delivered last week. I needed to start changing them out. I did inventory and cleaned the back storage room.

"Hey, Riah!" Ann said.

"Hey!" I said back.

"You okay? You look pale?"

"Yeah, I'm feeling a little under the weather, but I'll be fine.

"No, go ahead and go home. I need you well for next week. The All-star game will have bitches flying in here for a new look."

I got my things and headed home. I looked at my phone, and Fizz was calling again. I didn't feel like being bothered with him at the moment. All I wanted to do was sleep. I didn't have to work again until next week, so I was going to sleep all day. I had scheduled my first appointment for Monday. I was nervous as fuck. My mom said Fizz needed to be there, but what did she know? I got home, laid down, and dozed off. The baby was already doing a number on my body.

$\mathcal{A}$ whole month went by, and I still hadn't got through to Riah. I was about to just say fuck it, but something was telling me to just keep trying.

This chick who brought her car to get painted asked for my number. She was cute, but to be hood with it, she was too rough acting for me. I would fuck the shit out of her, though. I needed to talk with Riah and see if I could fix it, before I made that move, though.

I was walking into my mom's crib. I could smell the bacon.

"Just in time!" I said, as I walked in. I kissed her cheek, went to wash my hands, and came back and sat down.

"How you doing, ma?"

"I'm doing well. The doctors say I'm still cancer free, so I've been doing great."

"That's good to hear," I smiled at her.

"So, what's wrong?" she asked.

"What you mean?"

"Boy, who you think you talking to?"

"Mom, I don't know what to do. I called, texted, sent flowers, and popped up at Riah's apartment. She still won't respond to me."

"Oh that's what you're so depressed about."

"I wouldn't say depressed, but you know…"

"Boy, hush. Look at you… looking rough. You need a haircut."

"Damn, Mom, really? Tell me how you really feel."

"I just did, but you need to make her believe you. She still loves you. That's all she talks about when she's here."

"She still comes here? When?"

"I'm not telling you."

"Mom, you are obligated to be on my side."

"Boy, I'm not obligated to be on anyone's side but God, but I'll tell you this. Keep going to her apartment. When you see her, you'll get your answer."

"My answer to what?"

"Just try catching her before she leaves the house."

"I love you. I'm going to head there now. Pray for me. It seems like God listens to you," I said and hugged her.

"He listens to you, too. You just have to ask for the right things."

I left and decided to get a haircut. I needed to look good. Mom was talking about I looked rough.

I let Nikki get me together. I went home, showered, and got fresh from head to toe. I put on the cologne she always said she liked. I walked out the house and headed to get my woman back. I felt like she would be at home, out of all days. I told Sir to stop watching her after Nikki said I was a stalker.

I pulled right up to her apartment. Her car was outside, so I knew she was there. I got out the car, walked up the steps, ready to knock on the door right before she opened it.

Riah

$\mathcal{I}$ studied so long and hard for my test today that I fell asleep right on my books. I woke up and saw that I had missed calls. One was from Joyce, and one from my mom. I would have to call them later. The others were from Nikki, Deedee, and Mina. They knew I had class today and needed to study. After working so much for Ann, I was still exhausted. She was right about bitches coming in her store for All-Star weekend. She gave me a few days off to study, and I was glad she did.

I called Deedee back and talked with her. She said that she and Dozer were going to Jamaica for the weekend. After the All-Star party, he promised her a trip. I was happy for her and jealous. I always wanted to go to Jamaica. She said if I got my act together, I could be going with Fizz. I laughed at her. I was going to tell everyone this weekend that I was pregnant. That would give me enough time to tell Fizz first and get it over with.

I was about to shower when Ronnie called.

"Hey, Ronnie."

"Hey, beautiful. Did you have a good nap?"

"Yes, right through my studying," I laughed.

"We should go see a movie this weekend!"

"We can, but I plan to tell everyone about the pregnancy this weekend. I haven't decided when or where yet."

"Okay, well just let me know. Call me after class."

"Okay, thanks for checking on me."

"No thanks needed. Talk to you later."

I decided to go over my notes one more time. I was really trying to ace that test. I got up, ate some fruit, and laid down on my bed next to my clothes. I forgot I needed gas. I had about an hour, so I drove to the gas station with my sweats on. My hair was wrapped, so I looked decent enough to be out in public.

"Riah?" I heard someone say behind me.

"Mo?"

I hadn't seen him in so long."

"How you been?" he asked.

"I've been going to school and working. That's about it. How about you?" I answered and waited for his answer. I was happy I had that big sweater on, because I didn't want him to see I was pregnant.

"I've been busy with practice and classes."

"I bet. I've been hearing your name around town. You're doing your thing. I'm proud of you," I mentioned.

"Thanks. I hope I didn't start anything between you and ol' boy?"

"No, you didn't. We're past that now."

"Good, well I tried contacting you, but I'm guessing you changed your number?"

"Yeah I did. It's probably best, you know?"

"Yeah I know. Well nice seeing you, and I'm glad to still be alive," he said and smiled.

"Me too," I said, as I walked away. I paid for my gas, pumped, and left.

I got home and through that hot ass sweater off. I still had about thirty-five minutes before class. I laid down, resting.

I was planning on only being sleep for fifteen minutes. I slept for twenty-five. I hurried and got dressed. I was rushing, so I forgot the sweater I used to cover my pregnancy. It was hot as hell anyway. I would just have to wait until I put my chef jacket on in class because I had to go and didn't have time to find where I put the sweater.

I rushed out the door. As soon as I looked up, Fizz was right there. He was looking so damn fine that I dropped my books that I had in my hand. I knew I should've grabbed that sweater. His eyes roamed down to my stomach, and I noticed when they got wider.

"You pregnant?" he asked. I didn't answer him right away. I wasn't expecting for him to be on my doorstep, asking that. He turned and walked away.

"Fizz, wait! I was going to tell you."

He stopped in his tracks. He turned around slowly, looking at me.

"You think I want to hear that you're pregnant by another nigga?"

He continued walking away.

"It's yours!" I blurted out. He turned around so damn fast. I knew he was going to be pissed. I was three months, and he was just finding out.

"You better hope you just found that shit out today," he scolded.

TO BE CONTINUED

Looking for a publishing home?

Royalty Publishing House, Where the Royals reside, is accepting submissions for writers in the urban fiction genre. If you're interested, submit the first 3-4 chapters with your synopsis to submissions@royaltypublishinghouse.com.

Check out our website for more information: www.royaltypublishinghouse.com.

Text ROYALTY to 42828 to join our mailing list!

To submit a manuscript for our review, email us at submissions@royaltypublishinghouse.com

Text RPHCHRISTIAN to 22828 for our CHRISTIAN ROMANCE novels!

Text RPHROMANCE to 22828 for our INTERRACIAL ROMANCE novels!

Get LiT!

Download the LiT eReader app today and enjoy exclusive content, free books, and more

Do You Like CELEBRITY GOSSIP?

Check Out QUEEN DYNASTY!
Visit Our Site: www.thequeendynasty.com

CPSIA information can be obtained
at www.ICGtesting.com
Printed in the USA
LVHW031717241019
635246LV00010B/250/P

9 781542 994514